"THIS IS A [ ]

"Do you real[ ]sked.

"Of course I like it," JoBeth snapped. "Why shouldn't I? Someday I'll probably even run a museum just like this."

"That ain't what you ought to be doing right now, though."

JoBeth felt like screaming. Just what she needed: one more person who knew what was good for her. "And I suppose *you* have a better idea?" she asked tartly.

"Yeah. I wanted to tell you that . . . well you ought to be out in the sunshine learning how to ride that little yellow horse of your sister's."

"What would that prove?"

"That you could. Ain't that enough?"

"I went to a camp once where they were supposed to teach people how to ride," JoBeth admitted. "I didn't learn anything. Only how to fall off."

"Well, my offer still stands," Luke said softly. "If you wanta learn to ride your sister's horse, I can teach you how. . . ."

WHEN THE GOING GETS TOUGH

☐ **THEO AND ME by Malcolm-Jamal Warner.** TV's top teen star (Theo Huxtable on *The Cosby Show*) talks straight with teens about the problems they share—drugs, sex, school, friendship, parents, race, depression—in language that they use and understand. "Strong, helpful, solid advice . . . without sounding preachy."—*Publishers Weekly.*
(162161—$3.95)

☐ **THAT SUMMER by Janet Appleton.** When a protected, proper girl moves out on her own, she discovers life and love. It was the summer a girl became a woman. . . . "Tender, tragic, funny."—*Milwaukee Journal*
(164709—$4.95)

☐ **GOODBYE, PAPER DOLL by Anne Snyder.** Seventeen, beautiful and bright, Rosemary had everything. Then why was she starving herself to death?
(168305—$3.95)

☐ **THE TRUTH ABOUT ALEX by Anne Snyder.** What does a guy do when he's straight and finds out his best friend isn't? Brad was faced with two choices—standing by his friend and losing a West Point appointment, or giving in to the disapproving pressure from his family, girlfriend, teammates and the whole town. . .
(149963—$2.75)

☐ **MY NAME IS DAVY—I'M AN ALCOHOLIC by Anne Snyder.** He didn't have a friend in the world—until he discovered booze and Maxi. And suddenly the two of them were in trouble they couldn't handle, the most desperate trouble of their lives. . . .
(161815—$2.95)

☐ **ABBY, MY LOVE by Hadley Irwin.** Abby was keeping a secret about her father she should never have kept . . . "Poignant . . . eloquently written . . . sensitively deals with incest . . . an important book."—*School Library Journal*
(145011—$2.50)

Prices slightly higher in Canada

Buy them at your local bookstore or use this convenient coupon for ordering.

NEW AMERICAN LIBRARY
P.O. Box 999, Bergenfield, New Jersey 07621

Please send me the books I have checked above. I am enclosing $_____
(please add $1.00 to this order to cover postage and handling). Send check or money order—no cash or C.O.D.'s. Prices and numbers are subject to change without notice.

Name_____

Address_____

City _____ State _____ Zip Code _____
Allow 4-6 weeks for delivery.
This offer, prices and numbers are subject to change without notice.

THE
STONE PONY

by
Patricia Calvert

A SIGNET BOOK

SIGNET
Published by the Penguin Group
Penguin Books USA Inc., 375 Hudson Street,
New York, New York 10014, U.S.A.
Penguin Books Ltd, 27 Wrights Lane,
London W8 5TZ, England
Penguin Books Australia Ltd, Ringwood,
Victoria, Australia
Penguin Books Canada Ltd, 10 Alcorn Avenue,
Toronto, Ontario, Canada M4V 3B2
Penguin Books (N.Z.) Ltd, 182–190 Wairau Road,
Auckland 10, New Zealand

Penguin Books Ltd, Registered Offices:
Harmondsworth, Middlesex, England

Published by Signet, an imprint of New American Library,
a division of Penguin Books USA Inc.

This is an authorized reprint of a hardcover edition published by
Charles Scribner's Sons. A hardcover edition was published simultaneously
in Canada. Copyright under the Berne Convention.

First Signet Printing, December, 1983
14 13 12 11 10 9 8 7 6

Copyright © 1982 by Patricia Calvert
All rights reserved. No part of this book may be reproduced in any form without the
permission of Charles Scribner's Sons. For information address Charles Scribner's Sons,
a division of Scribner Book Companies, 866 Third Avenue, New York, New York 10022.

RL 6/IL 5+

REGISTERED TRADEMARK—MARCA REGISTRADA

Printed in the United States of America

PUBLISHER'S NOTE
This is a work of fiction. Names, characters, places, and incidents either are the
product of the author's imagination or are used fictitiously, and any resemblance to
actual persons, living or dead, events, or locales is entirely coincidental.

BOOKS ARE AVAILABLE AT QUANTITY DISCOUNTS WHEN USED TO PROMOTE PRODUCTS OR SERVICES.
FOR INFORMATION PLEASE WRITE TO PREMIUM MARKETING DIVISION, PENGUIN BOOKS USA INC.,
375 HUDSON STREET, NEW YORK, NEW YORK 10014.

If you purchased this book without a cover you should be aware that this book is
stolen property. It was reported as "unsold and destroyed" to the publisher and neither
the author nor the publisher has received any payment for this "stripped book."

For
Tana Patricia,
with love

Grief for a while is blind, and so was mine.

—Shelley,
Prometheus Unbound

1

Her. The word was still called a personal pronoun in Mechanics of English at Everly City High. But JoBeth Cunningham knew it would never sound as personal as it used to. A funeral changed so many things. Including the importance of pronouns.

Once, that word meant Ashleigh Susan Cunningham, named for a favorite aunt on Mother's side of the family. Five feet seven inches tall, one hundred and twenty pounds (a lot less at the end, of course). Eighteen years old, sky-colored eyes, hair the tangled, tawny gold of a lion's mane. Oldest daughter of Dr. Michael Cunningham, director of the Archer Museum of Art and History, and his attractive wife, Carol. Sister, of course, to JoBeth. Remembered fondly by all who'd known her.

I suppose if it'd been *me* who died, that's how I'd want to be remembered, too, JoBeth reminded herself.

But sometimes . . .

JoBeth sealed the letter her father had asked to

have mailed and put it in the "Out" box on the corner of his desk. She studied the handwriting on the envelope with satisfaction. It looked exactly like her own. The similarity wasn't an accident. She'd spent the past few months (started about the time Ashleigh got sick, hadn't she?) practicing the slope of his *l*'s, the tidy closing of his *a*'s, the dotting of his *i*'s, until now only a handwriting expert could've identified one script from the other.

It was probably one of those dopey things a skinny person with a pretty sister who was dying would do, JoBeth admitted to herself. She measured the size and sound of the words she'd use later to explain stuff like that to Robin when they met on the corner after work. The fact that she'd known Robin since first grade might make it easier to tell her that being glad Ashleigh was gone was not the same thing as wishing she'd never lived at all.

"Everyone thinks Ashleigh was the only one who was sick, Rob," she'd begin. She'd have to take a deep breath first, though, to make sure her voice didn't get that quivery note in it. It might. Four days after the funeral, for instance, she'd been sent down to the store to pick up some relish and mustard for supper—even if food didn't taste good anymore to anyone in the family, not hotdogs or hamburgers or anything. The clerk (wouldn't you know it'd have to be Ralph Smith's aunt?) had stared at her mournfully and tried to offer sympathy. JoBeth knew she ought to feel grateful that people cared, but when she tried to thank Mrs. Smith, her voice came out scared and squeaky, as if she'd been threatened rather than consoled. It was so unnerving she left change from a five-dollar bill lying on the counter.

Which meant she better watch Robin closely for any telltale signs of pity, too. Luckily they wouldn't be hard to spot. Robin didn't have a knack for wearing a mask over her feelings. That talent, JoBeth knew, was her own specialty.

"Well, Ashleigh *was* sick, and for a long time, too," she'd be quick to admit to Robin. JoBeth stared out the window beside her father's desk in the Archer Museum. "But now it's all over, Rob. For Ashleigh. For us. None of us will ever have to spend another afternoon watching her die."

Would that familiar "good-grief-what-should-I-say-now?" expression rise up in Robin's round, brown eyes? JoBeth hoped she'd pick words that didn't sound so hard, so heartless. She frowned and took a book from the shelf under the window. It was bound in burgundy leather, and its title was stamped in gold: *The Past and People of Ancient Luristan*. It was more than a hundred years old and had been written by an English scholar whose work Father admired very much.

JoBeth turned to the last chapter, the one about cuneiform symbols that had appeared on pieces of art found in Luristan. Some of the symbols were called pictographs because they were actually tiny pictures of the words they were meant to represent and were the earliest form of writing used by man. Such writing had originated in Sumerian settlements along the Tigris and Euphrates rivers more than five thousand years ago.

She'd only started to read the chapter yesterday, but surely among its many pages there would be a few words or letters that would help her decipher the script carved into the underside of a small stoneware pony displayed in one of the dioramas on the Lower Level of the Archer.

Thinking about the stone pony made JoBeth glance impatiently at her watch. Darn it. Still ten minutes to go before the museum closed. She sighed and began to leaf absentmindedly through the pages of the book.

It used to bother her that everybody was always so quick to agree that Ashleigh and Mother were alike as peas in a pod. On the other hand, they *were* alike—tall and tan and as athletic as a pair of citizens from some exotic island. When she got older, of course, JoBeth was able to convince herself she was just as lucky in her own way. After all, *she* was the one who'd run a museum someday, like Father; *she* would have diplomas from famous universities; *she,* like Father, would be the well-known author of many scholarly books about man's past.

"Kindred spirits . . ." That's what Father himself called the special bond they shared. JoBeth looked the word up as soon as he used it: ". . . kindred . . . of similar character," the dictionary assured her. To roll that phrase on the tip of her tongue always made JoBeth smile and feel warm inside. By comparison, the fact that Ashleigh loved horses and played tennis like a pro mattered less and less.

JoBeth stopped turning the pages of the book about Luristan. It occurred to her that Father hadn't used that phrase about kindred spirits for a long time. Not that its lack of use really changed anything at all. To love the Archer and its collected pieces of the past, to be as thrilled as Father himself had been when they'd unpacked that primitive stone pony almost a year ago—bonds like those could never be broken.

Or so it had always seemed. But what happened

4

twenty-one days ago might've changed everything. Forever.

To be the daughter who's left—maybe that's even worse than being the one who died, JoBeth suspected. She shifted her glance from the printed page to her arms. Freckles. She had them all over—arms, legs, back, nose. She never used to notice them. But when you'd been the second child in a family all your life and suddenly you got to be an only child, lots of things began to change—the importance of freckles along with the meaning of pronouns.

JoBeth trailed her fingers across her forehead. In fact, lately life seemed as full of puzzles as it was of freckles. An old anxiety had begun to nag at JoBeth again: Why would one child in a family be born golden and long-legged and happy, while a second one arrived thin and serious and as mixed up as a tourist who'd ended up in a town she never planned to visit?

Even Ashleigh's name had grace and glory in it! Her own—it was a shortened version of Josephine Elizabeth—was sometimes taken to be a boy's . . . maybe having something to do with the Book of Job in the Bible . . . even pronounced *Job*-eth!

JoBeth sighed. It was hard to concentrate on cuneiform symbols when your brain was in such a stew. What happened to Ashleigh, to be honest, didn't have anything to do with tourists who had freckles. What happened to her was the fault of the fourth sign of the zodiac. The sign of the crab. Some people called it the sign of cancer.

Cancer. It was a word JoBeth didn't like to say or hear anymore.

Six months ago JoBeth decided the ancient Greeks

hadn't suspected how terrible the crab would turn out to be when they gave its name to the zodiacal period between June 21 and July 22. In legend, the poor crab didn't do anything worse than pinch Heracles when he battled the Hydra. But by the twentieth century, it'd come to be associated with grim changes in a person's blood cells, her spleen, her bone marrow.

A sound from the entryway made JoBeth lift her glance in time to see the last two visitors at the Archer leave through the oak doors that faced Grant Street and the Parkway.

Ashleigh's doctors, being scientists and all, never mentioned the zodiac when they spoke about her illness. "The name of your daughter's disease is acute lymphocytic leukemia," JoBeth overheard them tell her parents. They used a shorthand term for it, too: ALL, they called it. Once, Ashleigh tossed her lion's mane, winked, and tried to make a joke out of it.

"Hey, you guys," she quipped one afternoon when they were all together, "maybe departments and agencies and diseases can be described by their labels. Healthy people go to work for HEW, see? Smart ones spy for the CIA, okay? And if you get ALL—baby, that's *all!*"

She grinned bravely, and JoBeth remembered how square and white her teeth had been. But Ashleigh's eyes, eyes that were still the color of the sky, had been shiny with tears.

From the first days of Ashleigh's illness, JoBeth told herself the end was a thing out in space someplace. It wouldn't dare arrive, she was sure, until everyone in the family agreed they were ready for it. And when it did come, they would gather around Ashleigh's bed and hold hands, like when sad endings were shown on TV. JoBeth never imagined she might be alone with Ashleigh when that time came.

At the beginning of summer, she and Mother and Father went to the hospice to take turns sitting with Ashleigh for two hours at a time. One morning (it seemed like many of the others), JoBeth decided to sit closer than usual to the edge of her sister's bed. So I'll be right here in case she wakes up, JoBeth told herself. The truth was, Ashleigh had drowsed the clock around for several days in a row, as still and pale as a princess in a fairytale, her gold mane thin and dull from weeks of chemotherapy.

On the other afternoons, it'd been a lot different. Then Ashleigh had been restless and eager to talk. Several times she started her conversation with exactly the same words, too:

"Let me tell you how I made up the name for my horse, JoBeth. See, I thought it'd be neat if I used the same letters as . . ."

It was probably the medication she had to take that made Ashleigh talk so weird, JoBeth decided. Just the same, Ashleigh's words caused a peculiar dread to close its fingers around JoBeth's heart. It was as if Ashleigh wanted to confess some kind of secret, as if she knew tomorrow or the day after she might not be able to.

"You'll feel better tomorrow, Ash," JoBeth insisted. "You can tell me tomorrow." But Ashleigh didn't. Couldn't.

Because what happened next reminded JoBeth of something that had happened before Ashleigh got ALL. They'd been loafing and playing anagrams all afternoon at the cabin on Gull Lake; then, just before suppertime, JoBeth had watched her sister run to the end of the dock and dive off it.

Ashleigh had risen in the air as sleek as a dolphin and sculpted an arc against the summer sky with her body. Then the blue water had passed over her strong shoulders, bikinied hips, and long brown limbs as she vanished under the smooth surface of the lake with scarcely a ripple to mark her passing. She slipped exactly the same way into what her doctors called a coma.

"Coma," JoBeth repeated, and leaned her elbow against Ashleigh's bed. What a soft, pillowy word it was, c-o-m-a. But it meant for sure now there'd never be a way to find out what Ashleigh had wanted to tell her: *Let me tell you how I made up the name for my horse, JoBeth; I thought it'd be neat if I used the same letters as . . .*

JoBeth squirmed and tried to find a more comfortable way to sit on the hard-backed chair beside Ashleigh's bed. A hawthorn tree was in bloom outside the hospice window. Being on the main floor, able to see grass and trees close by, was one of the things that made a hospice a nicer place to be than a hospital, where sometimes a person got stuck up on the fifteenth floor and could see only sky.

But maybe the best thing about a hospice was that everybody knew why a person came to one. To die, that's why. Strange as it might seem, it made each day more cheerful, because nobody pretended anymore that it wasn't going to happen. At the hospital, the doctors and nurses had all been so determined Ashleigh would get well, would at least have another remission, and were so disappointed when she only got worse.

JoBeth decided it would be a good idea to spend

her two hours with Ashleigh concentrating on worthwhile things. Like how she'd miss her. Only it was hard to do; after all, Ashleigh wasn't really gone yet. JoBeth then tried to make a mental list of all the nice things they'd done together, things that would be important to remember when she got old. *She* would get old; Ashleigh would be golden and eighteen forever.

But the list was short. They'd been sisters, JoBeth began to realize, but never close ones. They'd just been too different. Being so different, there'd been nothing much to share. Oh sure, there'd been one time when she was ten and Ash was fourteen that they'd spent two weeks together at a girls' camp in Colorado.

Ashleigh had been crazy about it. JoBeth had despised every second. The beds at the camp were hard and the sheets were scratchy. Everyone had to eat hearty food like beef-and-barley stew, which JoBeth loathed. All the girls washed in cold mountain water every morning like pioneers. The camp brochure said such things as "built strong character." That wasn't the worst part, though; there hadn't been a library or a museum within miles.

JoBeth especially remembered a horse at the camp she was assigned to ride. He'd been a runty little thing with brown and white spots all over, not to mention a mind of his own. No sooner did she get on him than he took the bit in his teeth and flew as if he'd sprouted wings over a field of black-eyed Susans.

"Hang on, JoBeth, hang on!" Ashleigh's cry had reeled out behind her like a lariat but otherwise hadn't helped much. When the ground rose up to smack the breath right out of JoBeth, the flowers, which looked so soft from a distance, had been another disappointment. After that disaster, JoBeth had spent every morning in the kitchen at the main lodge with Mrs. Culpepper, the camp cook, and read to her out of a book called *Life in a Medieval Castle* she'd had the good sense to stick in her suitcase before the trip.

"Gracious me," Mrs. Culpepper had declared, smiling and covered to her elbows with flour as she rolled out biscuits for the noon meal, "I do believe you are the most unusual child I've met since I came to cook at Camp Bide-A-While fifteen years ago!"

Not as unusual as my sister Ashleigh, JoBeth had wanted to explain, but didn't. Boiling sun, flies, ticks, hard beds, cold water—none of that stuff ever bothered Ashleigh. She could do anything. And did. In junior high she even won first place in an 800-meter track event and got her picture in the paper.

"Local Miss Places First!" exclaimed the caption on the sports page. Mother had it framed, and the picture still hung in the music room beside a blue ribbon Ashleigh'd gotten for something else. When she was sixteen, only a year before ALL, she got her own horse for her birthday. The only time JoBeth had ever seen it was the day it was delivered to a stall at the Ohio Hunt and Show Club. It'd been so hot and sunny that afternoon, just like those horrible days in Colorado, and the air was noisy with flies.

"Don't make me come out here again!" JoBeth remembered wailing loudly, almost ruining the birthday celebration for everyone. Nobody did, either.

JoBeth glanced at her sister's bed. Ashleigh's hand lay palm upward on the smooth white sheet. On her wrist was a narrow plastic ID bracelet that gave her name and her blood type. Until she got sick, the only bracelet JoBeth ever saw on that wrist was a blue terrycloth sweat band Ashleigh wore when she went to play tennis with Mother.

Ashleigh's fingers were curled childishly inward, her thumb sheltered by the other four as if it were the occupant of some unusual seashell. JoBeth inched her own fingers slowly across the deserted white beach toward her sister's wrist. It had been years and years (or had she, ever?) since she'd held Ashleigh's hand. Blue veins showed through Ashleigh's skin, fine as rivers on a map. JoBeth threaded her way along those faint pathways with her index and middle fingers.

She felt a tiny electric jolt when Ashleigh's pulse printed itself against her fingertips. Oh, how frail it seemed! It was no more substantial than the heartbeat of a butterfly. And just like a butterfly, it was capricious ... flew off ... returned a moment later ... then was gone.

JoBeth waited.

A single, round, smooth sigh escaped from Ashleigh. The butterfly would come back. It had to. People didn't die in such a soft, quiet way. Not ones with eyes the color of the sky. The end was still out there in space someplace, waiting for permission to come on stage. Just the same, sweat dampened JoBeth's upper lip, the roots of her hair.

Outside, the sun kept on shining as if nothing unusual had happened. The wind pressed the blossoms of the hawthorne tree against the window pane. The insolent sound of a motorbike sounded on a distant street. Ashleigh's plastic bracelet brushed JoBeth's fingertips.

JoBeth, you ought to ring for a nurse.

Another nice thing about a hospice room was that it was furnished just like a person's bedroom at home. Just the same, JoBeth flinched when she caught sight of herself in the mirror above Ashleigh's maple dresser. In that book about life in a medieval castle poor Mrs. Culpepper had had to listen to, it said quite plainly that mirrors in deathrooms were not supposed to reflect images.

JoBeth, it's time to call someone.

They'd been so different as sisters that nothing JoBeth had ever done for Ashleigh seemed special. But now, oh, if only there was some small thing that would let Ashleigh know how much . . .

JoBeth remembered she'd once seen a pair of bandage scissors in the drawer of Ashleigh's bedside table. She opened the drawer. The scissors were still there. JoBeth picked them up. She snipped the plastic bracelet off Ashleigh's wrist and dropped it into the wastebasket beside the bed. She glanced down: it looked like a broken handcuff.

"There—you aren't a prisoner anymore, Ash," JoBeth whispered. "Not anymore. Not ever again."

JoBeth sat down and hung onto herself with thin, freckled arms. She rocked slowly from side to side and was careful not to glance in the direction of the mirror across the room.

JoBeth, you've waited long enough. Call somebody. Quick.

JoBeth decided it'd be best to wait until her tears started. She'd begin to cry any minute, now that Ashleigh was really gone. It would be a relief to have those tears, hot and honest, scald her cheeks and scour the dark corners of her heart.

JoBeth rocked and waited. Waited and rocked. She felt cool and alone. Her bones seemed no more than frail wires in her limbs. Her chest, the place where her heart was supposed to be, was a pale, round hole with nothing in it.

When the nurse stopped by on her regular rounds, JoBeth was still rocking and waiting. But no tears ever came.

2

"JoBeth, dear, be sure to lock up when you leave," Miss Malowan called from the hallway outside Father's glass-walled office. JoBeth groaned. Miss Malowan had called out the same instructions from the same spot in the hall every evening all summer.

JoBeth wondered what would happen if she called back: "What's the best way to lock up death, Miss M.? Should I stick it in one of the file cabinets under *D*?" But only Ashleigh would've had the nerve to call her Miss M.!

Besides, tonight was definitely not the right night for making such remarks. Miss Malowan, heaven forbid, might be inspired to sit right down and have a long talk about them. If she did, there'd be no time left over to go downstairs to the Lower Level where the stone pony was kept.

"I won't forget, Miss Malowan," JoBeth called back meekly.

Miss Malowan stepped forward and leaned her tall self around the door frame. She smiled. JoBeth sighed, pushed her glasses up on the bridge of her nose, and made an effort to smile back. She realized, almost as if her teeth were not quite connected to the rest of her, that her braces hurt.

That feeble effort to be polite was enough to tempt Miss Malowan into the office, however. She was the same age as Father—fifty-eight—had a Ph.D. in arch-eology just like he did, and wore her thick, gunmetal-gray hair wrapped around her head like a warrior's helmet. She had a bold nose, strong chin, and piercing eyes, which JoBeth long ago decided reinforced an Amazon image. But despite the fact that Miss Malo-wan had been Father's assistant at the Archer for as long as JoBeth could remember, she wasn't sure she'd ever get used to Miss M.

Maybe I'm turned off because it was Ashleigh who was always Miss Malowan's favorite, JoBeth thought. "My little golden girl!" Miss Malowan used to cry when both children came to visit the Archer as small girls. Then, fearing perhaps to make JoBeth feel neg-lected, she always added with fierce cheer: "And *you* are my little brown nut!" JoBeth squirmed. She still had a hard time seeing herself as a little brown nut, especially one belonging to Miss Malowan.

"How are things going these days, JoBeth?" Miss Malowan asked sympathetically. JoBeth knew exactly what *that* meant. Since the funeral, that's what it meant. She glanced down quickly to stare at the book about Luristan. From a faded photograph, the black-eyed face of a boy about her own age stared back at her.

"Like his ancestors, the famous 'lost horsemen of Luristan,' this lad still garbs himself in faded blue, homespun clothing," read the caption beneath the picture. JoBeth studied the words but couldn't concentrate on their meaning; her only wish was to have Miss Malowan out of the room, out the front door, and on her way home.

"Oh, just fine, Miss Malowan," she heard herself mumble into the pages of the book. "I'm going to meet Robin after work. Maybe we'll go to McDonald's or something. Things are . . ." JoBeth knew she was talking too fast and tried to slow herself down— ". . . they're getting back to normal, Miss Malowan, really they are."

"Well, I'm glad to hear that, JoBeth." JoBeth peeked up long enough to see Miss Malowan nod her warrior's helmet with hearty approval. "Everyone on the staff has been worried about you, dear. We all know that losing someone you love is never easy."

But did I really love Ashleigh? JoBeth wondered uncomfortably.

"On the other hand, JoBeth, life has to go on. Yes, indeed! Life has to go on." JoBeth imagined Miss Malowan clanked pieces of armor as she spoke. She was one of those people who never seemed depressed or defeated. The whole idea was depressing.

"Now, dear—about tomorrow," Miss Malowan went on in her invincible way, "you plan to be in early, I hope?"

JoBeth sneaked another look at her watch again and gritted her teeth. Her braces reminded her that tooth-gritting was a no-no. "Yes, Miss Malowan. I'll be here at eight for sure. I'll get the coffee started, too." Three tours were going to be visiting the Archer over the weekend; it meant the museum would be even busier than usual.

Then JoBeth realized with a sinking heart that for

some reason Miss Malowan was in no special hurry to be gone. A pensive look had softened her Amazon brow.

She wants to tell me how she felt about Ashleigh, JoBeth suspected. But I don't want to hear it. Not tonight. Maybe not ever. JoBeth snapped her book shut with a loud thwack.

"Guess I better get going too, Miss Malowan," she said brightly. Did Miss Malowan give her a fleeting, anxious look? JoBeth decided she'd been mistaken, for Miss M. seemed to take the hint and proceeded on her way down the hall. From the lobby she boomed a loud "Good-bye!" over her shoulder.

Funny, wasn't it? The funeral hadn't put an end to anything. Ashleigh gone was even more on people's minds than Ashleigh alive. Especially her own. JoBeth watched Miss Malowan march through the oak doors, was grateful when they clanked shut behind her. Nothing would bring Ashleigh back, but life had to go on. Miss M. said so herself. And on the Lower Level, in the gloom of the summer evening, the stone pony still waited.

JoBeth checked her watch the minute she heard Miss Malowan's car leave the parking lot. Good. The cleaning men wouldn't arrive for an hour. She could spend the whole time downstairs. JoBeth began to hum the theme from Tchaikovsky's *Pathétique*.

"Do me a favor, will you?" Robin had suggested two days ago. "Find some other famous tune to insult with your talent. What you do to that one is so morbid it oughta be against the law." Robin's voice had a smile in it, and she'd given JoBeth an easy, teasing elbow in the ribs as she spoke.

"Morbid, orbid," JoBeth remembered snapping. "I'm entitled, okay? My sister died three weeks ago from a bite by the fourth sign of the zodiac. I guess I can be morbid if I feel like it."

Robin looped an arm lightly across her shoulder and gave it a friendly squeeze. "Hey, Jo! Don't get so bent outa shape! I was only trying to, you know, make you feel . . . better." Robin's brown glance had been concerned and kind.

JoBeth stopped humming. She wished she hadn't been so rude to Robin. Robin only wanted to be a good friend. Lately, though, JoBeth wondered if having a good friend wasn't almost more than she could stand. I don't want a friend right now, she thought. Sometimes I think I'd rather be. . . .

Rather be what? Oh, it was so hard to think straight anymore! JoBeth took off her glasses and rubbed her eyes. Ashleigh never needed glasses, of course. Or braces. Along with being golden, she'd had twenty-twenty vision and perfect teeth.

JoBeth sighed, settled her glasses back in place on the bridge of her nose, tapped her pocket to make sure her notebook was there. She'd copied a half-dozen cuneiform symbols into it yesterday; it was too early to tell if they were the ones she needed. Well, she never promised herself the job of deciphering the script on the stone horse would be easy. That's not the reason she invented such a challenge in the first place. JoBeth picked a brass key from the rack beside her father's bookcase and began to hum softly to herself.

She was glad tomorrow was another three-tour Saturday. For one day she'd feel like she had a real job. When you're not quite fifteen, no one except your own father would hire you for a few hours each after-

18

noon. JoBeth knew her small salary came directly out of her father's pocket and knew why, too: a part-time job at the Archer was supposed to keep her mind off what was happening to Ashleigh—what had, in fact, finally happened. JoBeth stopped humming.

She snapped off the lights in the office and stepped into the hall where a moment ago Miss Malowan had stood. The dim glow of an Ohio dusk filtered through the bronze-tinted windows of the deserted museum. Robin was the only person who knew she often stayed on alone after Miss Malowan left in the evening. Father would be upset if *he* knew; it was best not to tell him. JoBeth shrugged herself into the amber silence as into a favorite old sweater. *Oh, it felt good to be alone!*

"But I sure don't know why a person'd want to go down there all by herself," Robin groaned when JoBeth told her about visiting the Lower Level every night. "The whole idea is creepy, Jo. Even in the daytime, museums seem so dead. . . ."

Robin regretted the words almost before they were out of her mouth, rapped her knuckles hard against her forehead, tried to apologize. "Listen, Jo, I didn't mean to . . ."

"Hey, it's okay, Rob. Really. I know what you meant. Now it's *my* turn to tell *you* not to get bent outa shape!" JoBeth tried to smile and return Robin's teasing poke in the ribs. "Anyway, Ashleigh *is* dead. The word is still in Webster's. There's no sense pretending it doesn't exist. Somebody in Everly'll probably even use it again sometime."

The marble stairs under JoBeth's feet, cupped and worn smooth from the passage of thousands of visitors' feet over the years, led down to a special world she loved better than any other at the Archer. The bannister under her right hand was cool and hard; the brass key in her left soon was slippery with perspiration. And maybe—just maybe—tonight was the night the stone pony would tell her what she wanted to know.

Three walls of the Lower Level of the Archer Museum had been built of stone. The fourth was made of sliding glass doors that opened onto a sunken garden filled with relics of Italian statuary and *stele*, or remnants of ancient Greek ceremonial columns. In the center of the courtyard, draped with ivy, was a marble fountain out of which rose a dimpled nymph who spouted streams of water through smiling lips.

At the end of the garden a bank of stairs led up to the street level and to the employees' parking lot on the corner. It was nearly eight-thirty, and JoBeth saw that the garden had become a deep bowl into which blue summer darkness was being poured. Not that it mattered: It was not the garden that drew her back night after night to the Lower Level.

Along the wall opposite the glass doors, in niches designed especially for them by Dr. Cunningham, were the museum's dioramas.

"A Journey Through Man's Past" was what he called their many scenes. The smallest diorama, JoBeth's favorite, showed the province of Luristan in the ancient empire of Persia. The savage Zagros Mountains, which surrounded Luristan and once were the home of the lost horsemen, had been painted on the curved back wall of the diorama. It was in the Zagros, a chain of mountains stretching a thousand miles from the Black Sea of Russia to the Persian Gulf, that a young Michael Cunningham completed his work for a Ph.D. in archeology.

"I'll never be so old that I'll forget what it was like to climb the Zagros," JoBeth had heard her father say many times. "On those mountain tops, JoBeth, I felt close enough to heaven to pick the stars out of Orion's belt!" JoBeth wondered if that young man of twenty-five had been as handsome as the one she knew now. She wished she'd known her father then. They would've been such good friends, would've understood each other so well!

JoBeth had long ago memorized the names of the three bright stars in Orion's belt—Mintaka, Alnitam, and Alnitah. To repeat them to herself at night like a chant (once she'd overheard Robin say her *Hail Marys* and *Our Fathers;* was it kind of the same thing?) made JoBeth feel that she was forging another link in that bond of characteristics she shared with her father.

JoBeth frowned as she studied the mountains in the diorama. She remembered only too well how she'd hated those mountains in Colorado. But painted mountains are different, she decided. Inside the diorama no winds blew, after all. No bees filled the silent air with their droning. No birds sliced the sky with wings bold as knives. And best of all, in a miniature meadow made from dried grass and stones carved out of styrofoam but painted to look like granite, stood the stone pony.

JoBeth leaned toward the glass that enclosed the diorama. Her reflection, wavy in the dim light, came closer, closer: smooth brown hair cut short and worn like a cap, faint glint of spectacles, gray eyes behind them shy as a fawn's, until the image melted into her eyes when she rested her forehead against the cool glass of the case.

The stone pony was only inches from her nose. "A

charming artifact," Father called it the day they unpacked it. "No great work of art, mind you; nevertheless, it's an interesting example of the craft of the lost horsemen."

JoBeth knew no archeologist had ever been able to account for the strange disappearance of the people who, centuries before the birth of Christ, had inhabited the high meadows of Luristan. There were many theories, of course: a plague had taken their lives; they'd been seized by unknown invaders and sold into slavery; they'd left their harsh mountain homeland voluntarily to search for more agreeable surroundings.

Only one thing had been clear: the people of Luristan had raised horses, and they'd left relics in burial mounds scattered throughout their grassy meadows that told of their love for their steeds— beautifully-crafted bronze rein rings and bridle ornaments and saddle decorations, and occasionally, a small clay statue no more than three inches tall, just like the stone pony.

Even though he'd called it no great work of art, JoBeth could see that her father was enchanted by the stone pony, too. He turned it over and over in his palm, studied it as a lesser man might've examined a handful of precious stones. When her father smiled, JoBeth watched tiny lines make little fans at the corner of his eyes.

To make him proud of me—that's all I ever want! JoBeth thought.

"The horsemen of Luristan were called *derebeys*, or lords of the valley, by Assyrians and Hittites who invaded their mountain kingdom," Dr. Cunningham explained, interrupting her fantasy. "Those invaders

22

didn't come to plunder storehouses of gold and silver, however. They came to rob the *derebeys* of a different kind of prize—horses that looked like this little fellow, JoBeth, horses bred for endurance, with hearts as big as the mountain meadows they'd been born in."

He held the statue aloft for her to see. "Look at that strong back, JoBeth! Notice that well-shaped head! No wonder he was sought after."

JoBeth peered at the stone horse through the curved glass of the diorama. It was true: he looked strong and hardy and dependable. She always got a weird feeling, though, to realize he'd been shaped by a craftsman who'd been dead for thousands of years.

Before the clay of the statue's body had dried, his creator carved some marks on his underside. "More than likely those letters are a variant of cuneiform script," Father decided, "and when the artist was finished, the pony was probably fired in a kiln along with stoneware pots and water jars." Since the clay had not been glazed, the horse remained a common yellow-gray color and appeared actually to have been carved from stone. He stood poised inside the diorama, near foreleg raised, off hindlimb thrust forward. His forelock was swept back from sightless eyes as if a mountain breeze had just lifted it.

"Someday," Dr. Cunningham sighed, "I intend to decipher those marks—if I can ever find the time." Then he gave JoBeth a conspiratorial smile. "And providing a certain aspiring young archeologist doesn't beat me to it, that is!"

JoBeth turned the key in the lock of the glass case. The sound echoed loudly in the quiet room and reminded her once again that only Father or Miss Malowan had the authority to open any of the dioramas. Nevertheless, JoBeth pulled the panel aside, reached in, and lifted the stone horse out of his meadow.

The statue's unglazed surface was rough to the touch. The edges of the carving on its underside felt sharp and fresh against her fingertips. JoBeth fished her notebook out of her pocket. She frowned. Even for a scholar of Father's reputation, cuneiform writing would not be easy to decipher.

JoBeth had already done enough research to know that over many centuries cuneiform writing—or writing composed of squiggly lines, geometric shapes, and tiny pictures which had been carved into damp clay with a wedge-shaped tool called a stylus—had been altered by everyone who used it. She was determined not to be discouraged. If she used the burgundy book upstairs as a starting point, plus others in Father's collection, she might somehow be able to unravel the meaning of the marks on the stone pony's belly.

"You won't keep your secret from me, will you?" JoBeth whispered to the statue. "Because if you share it with me, it will make me more of a kindred spirit with my father than ever before."

Then even Miss Malowan would be impressed! JoBeth ran an index finger down the pony's spine, along the tail carried high on a wind that no longer blew. The pony's mouth was open, as if to better take in deep breaths of cold mountain air. His blind eyes were focused on who? What? The vanished *derebeys*, JoBeth wondered, or a lost mate?

"And you're going to tell me, aren't you?" she crooned. "You're going to tell. . . ."

A noise upstairs startled JoBeth. She glanced guiltily at her watch. The cleaning men had arrived. She'd dreamed her whole hour away! She put the stone pony quickly back in his mountain hideaway and locked the glass panel. In the morning, before Miss Malowan came in, she'd put the key back where it belonged on the rack.

JoBeth sighed. Maybe it was just as well: Robin would be mad if she had to wait too long on the corner. One by one, JoBeth turned out the lights in each diorama. First, Cleopatra and her golden court fell into oblivion; next, a farming scene along the Yangtze River where papier-maché peasants harvested a field of rice was wrapped in gloom; last of all, the province of Luristan was delivered to darkness.

"I'd better hurry," JoBeth confided to the stone pony, "because I know Miss Malowan's right. Life has to go on. . . ." But lately, it was getting harder and harder for JoBeth to leave the Archer each evening.

"One of these nights I won't leave at all," she said out loud. She'd already made some plans: she'd hide in one of the closets on the third floor where the collection of Early American quilts was stored. In the evening after the cleaning men were gone, she'd sneak out to eat cheese and crackers and drink orange pop from one of the vending machines in the employees' lunch room. Afterward, she'd take the pony out of the diorama and work on her decoding project. "Then I'll be happy," JoBeth said aloud. "Alone and happy."

One night, when she was sure Miss Malowan was gone, she had climbed into Queen Victoria's long, low mahogany linen chest that was displayed in the English Royal Collection on the second floor. It might make a nice bed. . . .

But as she lay there, JoBeth realized it would be

quite possible for a person to wish herself right out of existence. She felt herself grow smaller, smaller . . . her bones began to dissolve in her limbs . . . the place where her heart was supposed to be once more became a pale, round hole.

Dumb, JoBeth chided herself as she climbed out of the chest, really dumbdumb*dumb*! Just the same, as she prepared to leave the Archer again, JoBeth couldn't resist a loving glance around the Lower Level: in this world, where fragments of the past were trapped in glass cages, no surprises waited for a person. All ends had long ago been accomplished. Grief was simply a *thing*, no more troublesome than the African death mask on the far wall, its mouth opened in a wordless wail of despair.

JoBeth hurried to the glass doors and stepped outside into the garden. In the summer dusk the statues and *stele* looked airier than by day. The climbing vines that grew along the garden wall (Miss Malowan called them bougainvillea) were fragrant on the evening air.

JoBeth ran quickly up the stairs that led to the employees' parking lot. She only looked back once.

Except for the two rooms on the main floor being cleaned, the museum was dark. Tomorrow night will be better, JoBeth promised herself. I'll work hard on those symbols and won't dream the time away. . . .

Ashleigh used to tease her about that with a sigh and eyes cast heavenward: "You worry me, Joey, you really do! Look at you. No meat on your bones, pale as a ghost, mildew in your eyebrows—always mooning over the past. 'And here she is, ladies and gentlemen, the World's Youngest Archeologist.' Let it go, Joey; come out to the stables with me today instead. . . ."

Sometimes JoBeth wished she hadn't always

refused Ashleigh's invitations. One thing for sure: Ashleigh sure liked that goofy horse. The name she'd given him was weird. It had something to do with hay or oats or some other kind of grain, didn't it? JoBeth could never quite remember what it was; she'd made a habit of tuning Ashleigh out every time she started to rave on about that dumb birthday present.

JoBeth unlocked her bike and wheeled it to the curb. She waited for the welcome glow of Robin's yellow ten-speed to materialize out of the twilight.

Hurry up, Rob; there's something I've been wanting to tell you only I never could find exactly the right words, but now I have, Rob, and I'm glad, see, that Ashleigh doesn't have to wear handcuffs anymore and that I can start to . . .

But was that *really* what she wanted to tell Robin? It was a warm night, but JoBeth shivered. The truth was, nothing that'd happened all year had been fair. Ashleigh had done everything so well—swim, play tennis, ride horseback. Being four years older meant she got to do everything first, too. Even die. Then, before she could swallow her words, JoBeth heard herself reproach the empty street with a regret that had haunted her all summer:

"Why couldn't it have been me?"

3

When the sleek yellow ten-speed blossomed out of the dusk moments later, Robin was not its rider. It was Charlie, Robin's brother, who halted the bike at the curb.

"Hi, JoBeth," he panted. When he got his breath and managed a wide smile, JoBeth marveled once again that Charlie LaPierre seemed to have more teeth than an ordinary person. In a dark room, she used to think, that smile would be worth at least a hundred and fifty watts. Then JoBeth realized she must be studying him in a peculiar fashion, for between exhausted puffs, Charlie carefully explained his appearance in place of his sister.

"Robin had to run across the street at the last minute to baby-sit the Dexter twins," he said. "Bucky cut his leg on the jungle gym, and Mr. and Mrs. D. had to haul him down to Emergency at St. Benedict's." Charlie gulped for air. "And you know those Dexter twins! There'd have been a real emergency at St. Ben's if they'd ended up down there with Bucky."

Charlie paused in his recital, and JoBeth realized he was regarding her with the same anxious look Miss Malowan had given her an hour ago.

"Rob tried to give you a jingle at the museum," he went on softly. "She didn't want you to be surprised when I showed up in her place. When you didn't answer the phone, she told me you must've gone downstairs already, that you do almost every night." He wrinkled his brow. "Isn't that a little spooky, kid?"

Charlie's eyes were brown like Robin's. Round and brown and kind. But why did he have to start wearing a beard? He used to have a nice chin with a dimple in it, like a movie star. Now you couldn't even see it for all the honey-colored fur that covered it up.

JoBeth moved her fingers uneasily around the handgrip of her bike. Charlie reached out and gently covered them with his own. "Hey, JoBeth, how come we never see you over at our house anymore?"

His tight yellow curls made JoBeth think of the bust of Alexander the Great that sat on Father's desk at home. But *this* Alexander was real: his cheeks were scarlet from his fast bike ride, and a shining drop of sweat clung to the end of his nose. A young man immortalized in marble Charlie definitely was not. "Don't you know you're practically the only person I could never beat at chess?" he teased.

JoBeth inched her fingers out from under his tanned ones. He was only trying to be helpful. Like Robin. Neither one of them knew she'd rather just be left alone. Pretending to be concerned about her already-smooth hair, JoBeth brushed it down with a gesture she hoped looked natural.

"Gosh, Charlie, I've been too busy lately to even think about playing chess. Father's got a shipment of bronzes coming from New York next week, and they'll have to be catalogued. And tomorrow, well, tomorrow I've got to go out to the stables to check on Ashleigh's horse, so . . ."

The sound of her voice was a surprise. It was rushed and thin and breathless—maybe because everything she'd just told Charlie was a lie.

The bronzes had arrived a month ago and had long since been catalogued by Miss Malowan. And the only reason she mentioned Ashleigh's horse was because the stone pony had been so much on her mind lately. Stone horses were *her* bag, after all. The horse in Colorado had convinced her that she didn't want anything to do with the real kind.

"It's good to know you're busy," Charlie said. "Want to know something else, too, JoBeth?" He paused. "I always wanted to tell you how bad I felt about ol' Ash." Ol' Ash, who'd never get old.

JoBeth wished Charlie would look someplace except right straight into her eyes. "I know how I'd feel if something bad happened to Rob—even if there've been a few times I wanted to wring her neck!" He spoke comfortably about wringing his sister's neck, as if that occasional wish was nothing to get excited about.

He can say that because he knows deep down he really loves Rob, JoBeth thought. But I've never been really sure that I ever loved Ashleigh.

Would Charlie understand, JoBeth wondered, if she explained about being relieved Ashleigh was gone? That it wasn't fair something like ALL had to happen to the family? That Mother and Father were different now, too?

Charlie braced himself with stiff arms against the

handlebars of his sister's yellow ten-speed. JoBeth had known Charlie since she'd known Robin; he was three years older than Robin and, like his sister, had always been on the chubby side. Now, JoBeth noticed, Charlie's arms were thinner and roped with muscle under his swimmer's tan. Only yesterday he'd just been the brother of her best friend, someone who'd been fun to play chess with. But he'd changed; a Charlie she didn't know had taken his place.

"Listen, Charlie, you don't have to . . ."

"Make sure a fair damsel gets home safely through the wicked streets of Everly?" he grinned. "Sure I do—I'm a gentleman, don'tcha know?" He gave her a sassy wink. The lashes that screened his dark eyes were thick and brushy. His lips, framed by his new beard, were as pink as if he'd just finished eating a cherry popsicle. Gentleman or not, he *did* look older. JoBeth decided she might've liked him better if he'd stayed young and plump.

She climbed on her bike, eager to get home and out of Charlie's sight. Her head felt light. Things—life—changed too fast. Some people died. Others grew beards when they really shouldn't have. Nothing stayed the way it was supposed to. JoBeth kept her eyes fastened on the street and peddled faster than she needed to. It was only fifteen blocks home. They didn't pass quickly enough to suit her.

If Charlie was offended, he took pains not to let her know. "Sure you won't play me a game of chess tomorrow?" he wheedled the minute they turned into the driveway. "Bet you a root beer I can beat you now!" Well, he ought to be able to, JoBeth thought. He was a science major who wanted to be a doctor, just like his father. If he couldn't beat a fourteen-

(soon-to-be-fifteen) year-old girl at chess, something was wrong.

JoBeth slid a glance Charlie's way. "Golly, I can't play you a game any time soon, Charlie," she said. "Tomorrow's a big day at the Archer, what with three tours coming and all. Then on Sunday morning, like I mentioned, I have to go out to check on that horse."

"Terrific. Why don't I come along with you? It'd be fun; I'd like to see Ashleigh's horse myself." Once invented, JoBeth began to suspect, that white lie about Ashleigh's horse was not going to be easy to let go of.

"Maybe next time, Charlie. I'll call you one of these days, okay? Right now I better get into the house. Mother and Father will be wondering what's kept me."

Charlie shrugged good-naturedly, reached out to give her wrist a final agreeable squeeze, then flew off down the driveway. Under the light of the street lamp on the corner the long muscles on either side of his spine stood out in sharp relief through his thin T-shirt. His jeans rode low enough on his hips to menace decency. He turned to wave good-bye. The arm he held into the air was slim and unfamiliar.

JoBeth walked her bike slowly into the darkened garage, lowered the door, and wondered if she ever wanted to see him again. Lately, a lot of things just seemed to take more energy than she had to spare. And she doubted that she would ever get used to his beard. Or the fact that he'd gotten so old.

The lawn chairs in the backyard looked frail and lonesome in the evening light. The croquet set that Father ordinarily would've put up at the beginning of summer was not in its usual place. Ashleigh had been the croquet freak; without her, no one else wanted to play.

The tall French windows that flanked each side of the fireplace in the music room were open, and a tinkling sound floated out to JoBeth. She turned; the inside of the room was rescued from darkness only by the dim light of a green Tiffany lamp Father had bought at a New York auction on one of his business trips.

Mother, who rarely played the piano (and then not very well, in JoBeth's opinion), sat on the piano bench and picked out a tune. JoBeth wracked her brain to think of the name of it. Ah. "Bridge Over Troubled Waters." The way Mother played it, it seemed more sweet than melancholy. Then Mother closed the cover over the piano keys and turned around.

"Don't worry, Michael," JoBeth heard her mother say. "Things will be all right again. I know they will." She'd always called him Michael. Of course he was not the kind of man anyone would call Mike, let alone Mick. Although he was slender and not quite as tall as Mother herself, he had a princely air that Mother used to say came from his Highland Scot ancestors.

Mother, JoBeth observed, was brown again. She'd played tennis every afternoon since the funeral—played with desperate enthusiasm, in fact. But it must've done what she wanted it to do, because now she looked strong and healthy. And when she raised her glance, JoBeth was stunned to realize how much alike she and Ashleigh really did look.

The resemblance made JoBeth's heart feel pinched. She shifted her glance to her father. He perched on the edge of the loveseat and faced Mother. He held his hands clenched tightly between his knees. He looked so reserved and self-possessed, exactly the way a descendant of Highland lords ought to look, and JoBeth felt pleased to think: And *I* am my father's daughter. . . .

She'd heard the phrase even before she understood what it meant. "Your little JoBeth is certainly her father's daughter, Dr. Cunningham!" admiring teachers had always been eager to report. "She's a natural student, never needs any prodding, and always has something worthwhile to share with her classmates. Not to mention the fact she has the most *marvelous* manners!"

JoBeth smiled to herself. In the dim lamplight of the music room, her father's hair was a silvery halo around his head. He said he'd begun to get gray at sixteen, had been quite silver at twenty-five. Each morning, JoBeth searched her own brown locks for her first silver strand.

"I know what you're trying to tell me, Carol," JoBeth heard her father murmur, "but there are times—and I guess tonight's one of them—when I feel like my whole world has caved in."

JoBeth felt her pleasure fade. Her heart began to race. She'd never heard exactly that sound in her father's voice before. It was like broken glass. Raspy. Harsh. She moved to one side so the edge of the window sash did not interfere with her view of the scene in the music room.

The she understood what was wrong. He's just like everyone else, JoBeth realized. He misses Ashleigh, too. It isn't enough that *I'm* still here.

To her dismay, her father began to cry. His cheeks were scarlet; his tears made silver tracks across those two bright patches. JoBeth watched as her mother held out a pair of strong, brown arms. Dr. Cunningham leaned forward from his perch on the loveseat, knelt in front of the piano bench, and buried his head in his wife's lap.

"It'll be all right, Michael," JoBeth heard her mother murmur. She was crying, too. "I promise you it'll be all right. It will, it will, it will." She repeated the words over and over, sing-songy and simple, the way someone might soothe a needy child.

JoBeth closed her eyes. She wished she hadn't seen any of it. She could hardly breathe. *Betrayed*. Why did that word leap instantly into her head? Father had been her best friend, but now he was . . . JoBeth moved blindly away from the window and rested her forehead against the brick wall beside the back door. The bricks were rough but still warm from the afternoon sun.

There'd been a balance in the family before Ashleigh died: Mother and Ashleigh on one side, she and Father on the other. Now she was on the outside, alone. Suddenly it seemed childish to believe it mattered at all if she ever decoded that script on the stomach of the stone pony. It would never make things the way they used to be.

JoBeth moved her forehead from side to side across the rough surface of the bricks. She was sure she felt her skin break. Back and forth; back and forth. When, where, how might it all have turned out differently? And how come she was still the only one who couldn't cry?

Munchie was waiting patiently at the back door when JoBeth opened it. She was old, nearly ten; the guard hairs on her muzzle were frosted with silver. Her bangs bounced when she jumped up to give

JoBeth an eager schnauzer greeting. JoBeth shoved the dog down, sorry to be rude, but desperate to get up the stairs as quickly as possible. She was too late.

"Is that you, darling?" Mother called. "We're in the music room, JoBeth." JoBeth glanced through the archway. Her parents had leaped apart. Maybe they'd been alarmed by their treachery, too.

"Miss Malowan wants me to come in early tomorrow, so I'm going straight to bed," JoBeth answered. Her voice was steady, calm. Father might've abandoned his composure; she refused to do the same. Then, from the darkness at the top of the stairs, she called down: "On Sunday I'm going out to check on Ashleigh's horse." A startled silence filled the music room.

"But the horse is being cared for by the staff at the club, dear," Mother assured her finally. "You don't have to. . . ."

"I know I don't *have* to," JoBeth said crisply. "I just want to, that's all." Her lie, invented moments ago to hold Charlie at arm's length, used again on her parents for reasons JoBeth couldn't fathom, claimed a life of its own.

JoBeth took off her clothes in the comforting darkness of her room. She fished a favorite nightgown out of the bottom drawer of her dresser. It was old; she'd gotten it when she was only ten or eleven. Tonight was one of those nights when it'd be nice to be ten or eleven again. The gown was too small in the shoulders but was soft as a cloud from many washings. It flapped agreeably against her shins when she crossed the hall and stepped into the study.

Of all the rooms in the whole house, the study was

JoBeth's favorite. It always smelled of Father's pipe smoke and was faintly sweet from the odor of the cut-up apple he put in his thermidor to keep the tobacco moist. The walls of the room were lined with books—not new books with shiny covers, but old ones with leather bindings that had been read many times. His reading chair was leather, too, studded with large brass nails, and the map on the wall behind his desk was one JoBeth never tired of looking at.

It wasn't one of those plastic-coated, slick maps like they had at school. It was very old; its parchment edges were frayed, and it showed how the world looked centuries ago. Then, there hadn't been a nation called Iran; its name was Persia, and the Zagros Mountains ran down its middle like a spine.

JoBeth traced the names of the ancient villages of Persia with her fingertip . . . Hamadan and Ahvaz and Isfahan . . . and near Shiraz was the famous mountain pass called The Persian Gates. Alexander the Great had hurtled through that pass in 331 B.C., had descended on Xerxes' palace at Persepolis and burned it to the ground. And once, Father himself had stood on a mountain peak nearby and picked stars out of Orion's belt. . . .

Then JoBeth remembered she'd been betrayed. Mother and Father had each other now. She had no one. From her father's desk JoBeth picked up the snowdome she and Ashleigh had given him long ago to use as a paperweight. She turned it upside down. Snow cascaded from the earth into the sky and settled lightly on a ceiling of stars.

My whole life is like that now, JoBeth thought as she watched the last flake vanish into the heavens. Upside down. Weird. Not normal anymore.

Or had her life somehow *always* been different? No. That was silly. The only reason it seemed messed up now was because Ashleigh had gone and died.

JoBeth's forehead felt warm. She dabbed at it with the hem of her nightgown. She peered at the fabric, hoping to see drops of blood there. There weren't any. She set the snowdome back inside the faint circle of dust that marked its place. Maybe everything would start to get better on Sunday morning.

That's when she would ride her bike out to the Ohio Hunt and Show Club to see Ashleigh's horse. She'd stand in front of it, that horse Ashleigh'd gotten the year before she got ALL, the horse whose name and color were always so hard to remember, and then maybe it would happen.

Maybe I'll cry, JoBeth hoped. Maybe then I'll be able to cry.

4

JoBeth couldn't remember the last morning she'd been up so early. Fog hung in the backyard and made Mrs. Dalrymple's house next door seem furry and far away. With Mother and Father still in bed and the house so silent, JoBeth decided she felt almost normal.

She put a cautious finger to her forehead. The flesh there was pebbled and raw, like the mat burn she got once in gym class. She tugged her dark bangs down as far as they would stretch.

Miss Malowan had wanted to know what'd happened, of course; JoBeth mumbled something about tripping over a lawn chair. Mother's curiosity yesterday had been defused with a story about falling against the marble fountain in the courtyard at the Archer. Father had been so bemused that he hadn't even noticed her forehead.

JoBeth poured a glass of orange juice and made herself two pieces of whole wheat toast. Munchie sat near her chair, eager to be noticed. JoBeth slipped the dog her crusts, rinsed her dishes, and closed the back door softly when she left the house.

JoBeth looked at the bricks beside the back door.

Would there be bits of flesh, shriveled and dry as tiny pieces of potato skin, clinging there? She was vaguely disappointed to see that the bricks looked quite ordinary.

Well, there were *some* things to be grateful for. Like thank goodness I didn't let Charlie come along! JoBeth thought as she pedaled down the driveway. To have anybody along this morning would ruin the importance of the occasion. In a peculiar way, it was like going to visit Ashleigh's grave—which JoBeth did not intend to do for a long, long time. But going to the stables—well, it would be just as personal in a way, but not so hard to do.

It was a three-mile ride to the Ohio Hunt and Show Club. The hour was early, so highway traffic was light. The view of the rolling hills that bordered the far side of the Ohio River and marked the beginning of the state of Kentucky had always been one of JoBeth's favorites. Those Kentucky hills were not as fierce and majestic as the Zagros, of course. On the other hand, it might be years before she had the courage to see those Persian mountains in person.

JoBeth slowed as she came abreast the Cuyahoga Boys' Correctional Facility. Everyone she knew called it CBF; it was another one of those labeled things Ashleigh might've laughed about. But neither she nor Ashleigh, being the well cared-for daughters of a famous museum director, had ever known a boy who'd actually been sent to such a place. JoBeth was relieved that on this Sunday morning the lawns of the institution were clean and green and innocent of boys who were getting corrected.

The Ohio Hunt and Show Club covered one hundred sculptured green acres along the Ohio River. A variety of bridle paths crisscrossed the acreage, and near the barns were gymkhana courses and a show ring outlined with crisp, whitewashed fences. When JoBeth arrived at the hunt club office ten minutes later, a plump blonde woman whose name tag identified her as Mrs. Wilson greeted her with a small frown.

"Are you a member of our club?" she asked. "I don't believe I've seen you here before."

"No, ma'am, I'm not a member. But, my sister . . ."

"Goodness, dear—I'm very sorry, but this is a *private* club." Mrs. Wilson pointed to a sign behind her desk that declared sternly in red letters: *Members Only!* "However, if you were thinking of renting a horse for an hour or for the afternoon, why don't you and your sister try the public stables out on Ridgeway Drive?"

"I mean, my sister *used* to belong to this club. Her name is—that is, her name was Ashleigh Cunningham."

Mrs. Wilson put a finger to her lips, dismayed. "I'm sorry I didn't recognize you, dear! I guess I only met you once. Let me see, I believe it was the day your sister's horse was delivered to the club. Please forgive me." She seemed genuinely stricken.

"That's all right; I understand."

"So!" Mrs. Wilson was able to exclaim cheerfully as soon as she realized club rules were not about to be violated. "You're planning to ride this morning, ah . . . I'm sorry, dear, I can't seem to remember your first name."

"It's JoBeth."

"Yes. JoBeth. Well, that's a nice name, too. Of course, I always loved the name Ashleigh! And your sister matched it in every way. Now, JoBeth, I am sure you are welcome to any of the privileges that your sister enjoyed at the club." She flicked quickly through a card file on her desk. "Let me see—yes indeed, your sister's membership was paid up through the end of the year."

"Oh, I don't plan to ride or anything like that," JoBeth hastily explained. "That was my sister's bag. My bag is—" Wouldn't it get too complicated if she tried to explain about decoding some script on the belly of the stone pony? "—I've got a summer job at the museum, and besides I don't think we'll keep the horse much longer. Everybody says it'd be a good idea to sell it, what with Ashleigh gone and all." No one had suggested anything of the kind. "You know how it is—life has to go on."

Mrs. Wilson almost glowed with approval. "Indeed it does, dear. Sad as your sister's death was, I'm glad to hear you're able to have such a mature attitude about it. But if you decide you want to saddle up after all, you might be pleased to hear you've got the whole place to yourself this morning. The only other person around is our new exercise boy who likes to come in early and get his work done before the club gets busy."

"Exercise boy?" JoBeth felt her interest in seeing Ashleigh's horse begin to fade.

"Yes, dear. You see, many of our club members like to have their horses kept up—which means having their horses worked out regularly when they can't ride the mounts themselves. It's best for the horse, too. Can you imagine how boring it must be to be locked up day after day in a sixteen-foot box stall?"

Until Mrs. Wilson mentioned it, JoBeth had never needed to think about the matter one way or another. She smiled in agreement while at the same time trying to keep her braces covered with her lips. Maybe the exercise boy wouldn't disturb her. Having nobody else around sounded like a blessing, though.

"Do I need a key or anything, Mrs. Wilson?"

"Only for the tack room, dear. Here it is. Ashleigh's locker in the tack room will correspond to the number on the door of her horse's stall. We don't lock the stalls themselves, of course. In case of fire, you know."

But JoBeth shook her head when Mrs. Wilson held the key out to her. "I won't be riding or anything like that, so I don't need . . ."

"Take it, dear, take it," Mrs. Wilson insisted, and pressed the key into her palm. "Horseback riding is a wonderful hobby. Good for the body and good for the brain, as they say. You might get down to the barn and have a sudden change of heart."

A change of heart, JoBeth thought. How surprised Mrs. Wilson might be if she knew that's exactly why I'm out here.

The rays of the early morning sun slanted through the high stable windows. Pigeons, feathered in iridescent blues and greens and bronzes, roosted in the ceiling rafters and cooed dreamily among themselves. Shafts of sunlight divided the aisle of the barn into diagonal sections that were grainy with alfalfa dust and oat chaff. The whole place smelled a lot cleaner and sweeter than the barn at Camp Bide-A-While, JoBeth decided. Just the same, as she walked slowly down the aisle, she felt a familiar tingle of dread.

She glanced down at the number on the key Mrs. Wilson had forced her to take. "Eighteen." JoBeth looked up at the number on the stall to her left. "Thirty-seven." It held a large roan horse with white, rolling eyes. Ashleigh's horse, then, must be in a stall about midway in the barn.

JoBeth proceeded slowly. It was a way to delay the moment when she'd have to face Ashleigh's horse. Some of the stalls along the way were empty. One of them housed a tall, sorrel horse whose name plate identified him as Sudden Fame. He trumpeted cheerfully as she passed by. JoBeth shuddered. If Ashleigh's horse turned out to be that tall or that noisy . . . it was probably a dumb idea to have come out here.

All the stall numbers on the right side of the aisle were even. Fourteen, sixteen, eighteen . . . JoBeth's palms were damp, and the key to the tack room felt slippery. It reminded her how nervous she'd been the first time she opened the diorama case.

She waited in front of stall number eighteen for several minutes. Fear climbed through her as neatly as a thief through an unlocked window. The interior of the stall was dusky, and JoBeth couldn't make out the color of the horse inside. She could only sense one *was* there. She walked cautiously up to the stall door. It was wood on the bottom half and screened with stout wire mesh on the top. A small brass plate tacked to the wooden part informed her:

Riono
OWNER: Ashleigh Susan Cunningham.

Riono. Of course. It was the name she'd tried to remember two nights ago, the one that had something to do with some kind of grain. Ashleigh pronounced the name Rye-o-no. Rye was a kind of grain people used to make a dark, flavorful bread. In fact, that's exactly what Ashleigh always called him: just plain old Rye.

JoBeth stood on her tiptoes and pressed her face against the wire mesh that separated her from the horse. She drew back hastily; her forehead still tender. She could hear the horse move his feet restlessly in the straw. She slipped the catch on the stall door, slid it back, and eased herself inside.

"Rye?" she called timidly. "That's a good boy, Rye; here Rye. . . ."

The horse moved out of the shadows toward her. A bar of sunlight slanted across his face, which appeared to be a dark, smoky color. His eyes, large and set well out in their sockets, fixed her with an unfathomable stare.

"You're disappointed, aren't you?" JoBeth whispered. She didn't blame him. "You were expecting Ashleigh—but got me instead."

By way of reply, the horse snorted softly. His warm breath dampened the knuckles of her left hand. JoBeth wondered if he was recording the smell of her somewhere inside his smoky head. He pressed his muzzle against her chest and gave her a gentle shove.

Panic gripped JoBeth. Perspiration trickled like beads of ice water down her ribs. She started to breathe too fast. Ashleigh's doctor called it hyperventilation. The first time it happened, JoBeth had been at the hospice. "Slow and easy, JoBeth," Dr. Wainright advised. "Remember to breathe slow and easy." But why was she hyperventilating now? This was a horse, not a hospice.

Horses had always scared her, though. That brown and white runt at Camp Bide-A-While hadn't been the first one. Those fiery, glass-eyed steeds on the merry-go-round at the state fair the year she was six had been even worse when they whirled round and round, lashed to a frenzy by the calliope music, nostrils red-lined, mouths agape with desperate effort.

JoBeth remembered she hadn't wanted to ride the merry-go-round that afternoon, had begged softly not to have to. Mother pushed her forward anyway, with promises of how wonderful it was going to be. Ashleigh had grabbed her up, heaved her across a midnight-colored horse with diamonds in his bridle, had forced her fingers around the gleaming, ferruled pole in front of her.

"Ride, Joey, ride!" Ashleigh cried merrily over her shoulder as soon as she leaped onto a horse in the next row that was the color of fire. "Oh, it's wonderful, Joey—I feel like I'm flying, flying!"

But no matter how loud the calliope shrieked or how hard JoBeth's horse tried to catch up, Ashleigh stayed in the lead on her red one, her own tawny mane streaming behind her like a banner. Soon the colors of the crowd were stirred to a blur . . . the shrill music made JoBeth's fingertips numb . . . and when the ride was over, she upchucked her hot dog and cotton candy all over her new green shorts.

"Oh, Bethy, poor baby," Mother had crooned, contrite, "you've just had too much excitement for one day."

No, no, JoBeth wanted to scream, *it was the horses, the horses!* Couldn't anyone else see it, too? How their hearts were breaking, that no matter how fast they ran it never did any good, they still could never catch up? They just had to keep running harder and harder until their hearts broke.

The only horse JoBeth ever liked at all was the

stone pony. He was cool and silent and safe. The one in front of her right now was as scary as any of the others had been. JoBeth backed up slowly, braced herself against the door, fumbled for the catch. She felt dizzy, just like the day she'd flown over that field of black-eyed Susans. She held out a hand to break her fall.

Instead of falling, she laid her palm flat against Rye's thick neck. The muscles under his smooth, silky hide were hard and resourceful. And warm. The stone pony had always been so cool. JoBeth tried to breathe slower, as Ashleigh's doctor had suggested. She swallowed and tried to compose herself. Weren't horses supposed to like to have their ears rubbed?

Sweating, JoBeth moved her hand upward from Rye's neck to his face, his cheek, his ear. He sighed and his eyelids drooped with pleasure. The key to the tack room was still slippery in her other hand. *A change of heart,* Mrs. Wilson had suggested.

"Hey, horse, do you w-w-want to go for a r-r-r-ride?" JoBeth heard herself stammer.

The words hung on the air. She must be crazy! She didn't know how to ride. Only how to fall off. Or barf up a hot dog. Besides, wasn't it wishful thinking to imagine that mounting Ashleigh's horse would make her cry? On the other hand, Mrs. Wilson said there was no one at the club yet. Which means, JoBeth realized, there's no one around to see how clumsy I am, that I am the most beginning of all beginners.

JoBeth backed out of Rye's stall. "Don't go away, horse," she called over her shoulder, and went to look for the tack room.

JoBeth discovered that in the tack room each club member had been assigned a large, ventilated wooden locker in which was kept all of his or her riding gear and grooming tools. In Ashleigh's, there was even a pair of crimson jogging shorts. JoBeth lifted Ashleigh's slim, flat saddle from its wooden tree, picked the bridle off its wood peg, and stuffed her pocket with some colored pellets out of a cardboard container labeled Horse Yummies.

JoBeth Cunningham, you've got to be a grade A dreamer, she told herself as she lugged the saddle back to stall eighteen. You were only ten years old the last time you watched anybody saddle a horse—and even then you weren't really paying attention. You were thinking about how soon you could get home and back to the museum and your books. So what makes you think that now you can manage to get this saddle on Rye—much less ride him?

It was a goofy thing to try. Just the same, something inside JoBeth made her determined to do it. Afterward, when Rye was saddled and bridled, JoBeth admitted to herself that he'd almost gotten himself dressed for the occasion. He actually seemed eager to let her put the bit into his mouth, almost shrugged himself under his saddle. Then, when JoBeth led him out of his stall and into the aisle of the barn, she was able to see for the first time what color he actually was.

To her amazement, Rye wasn't smoke-colored all over. His body color, she decided, was a mellow yellow—or just about the color of oatmeal after you'd sprinkled it with a little brown sugar and poured lots of thick cream over it. But his mane and tail were a soft charcoal color, just like his face. His legs were dark up to the knees, and there was a faint charcoal-colored stripe all the way down his spine.

Most surprising of all was Rye's size. Ashleigh had

been such a tall, leggy girl, and it seemed natural to expect she'd have chosen a tall, leggy horse to match. Instead, Rye was a compact, deep-chested horse whose withers were just about even with JoBeth's chin.

A shadow fell across the open door at the end of the barn. JoBeth felt her heart leap. Someone in a blue shirt rode briskly past.

"Darn it!" she groaned out loud. She'd really counted on having the place all to herself. It seemed important to be alone to take this one—and only— ride on Ashleigh's horse. It was an experience that should be perfect and private. JoBeth was tempted to turn around and forget the whole thing. But Rye *was* saddled; more than that, JoBeth saw the horse gaze longingly past her to where the lemony summer sunshine spilled on the ground beyond the doorway. His ears were pricked forward in anticipation.

"Okay, okay, horse, I get the message," she sighed. Like Mrs. Wilson explained, it must be pretty boring to be cooped up day after day in a sixteen-by-sixteen foot box stall. JoBeth tried to firm up her courage by gritting her teeth. A stab of pain reminded her that it was still a bad habit for anyone who wore braces.

By the time she'd walked Rye to the barn door, the horseman in the blue shirt had vanished. Good. JoBeth gathered the reins over Rye's neck, as she remembered being taught in Colorado, and stuck her left foot in the stirrup. The first time she tried to mount, she couldn't make it up. Not the second time, either. She looked around for a mounting block. They had one in Colorado for the girls who were extra short. There was no mounting block to be seen. Finally, by boosting herself as hard as she could on the

ball of her right foot and grabbing a fistful of mane
she hauled herself topside.

JoBeth congratulated herself and collected th
reins. She pressed the calves of her legs nervously int
Rye's side while visions of black-eyed Susans bloome
in her head. But Rye simply moved forward with .
civilized step and headed for a winding cinder bridl
path marked by a wooden sign that read *Mountai*
View. Maybe it was one of the trails he and Ashleig
often used, JoBeth thought.

Through a screen of willow and alder leaves
JoBeth could see once more the placid Ohio River an
beyond it the soft green hills of Kentucky. She coul
also plainly see the rider who'd passed by the bar
door a few minutes before.

He was a boy about her own age, very thin, and th
light breeze pressed his blue shirt flat against his nar
row chest. He was maneuvering a tall bay horse wit
four white socks and a blaze on its face over a series o
long, painted poles that had been laid about four fee
apart in a straight line on the ground.

With any luck I can turn back before he sees me
JoBeth thought. Then I'll look for a different trail t
take .... He was probably the exercise boy Mrs
Wilson mentioned. Just then, to her dismay, Ry
whinnied a greeting to the bay horse with the blaze
face.

The bay lifted his head and whinnied a lively reply
His rider turned in the saddle. The boy was darkl
tanned and his eyes, deep set and seen from such a
distance, looked like two empty black holes in his face
He seemed hauntingly familiar. As JoBeth racked he
brain to think who he reminded her of, she was struck

50

by his attitude of wariness. He was as tense as a fox who'd caught the scent of hounds.

Then it dawned on JoBeth that the boy was studying her as sharply as she studied him. As if he'd come to a decision, he lifted one hand in a slow wave. He rose lightly in his saddle, put the big bay horse into a trot, and headed briskly in her direction.

JoBeth froze. He'd want to talk. Might be a tease, too, like Charlie. Maybe he'd wink and act smart. The morning, which was to have been so special, was suddenly ruined. JoBeth wheeled Rye as hard as she could and went straight back to the barn.

"Why can't people ever learn to leave other people alone?" she muttered as she unsaddled Ashleigh's horse. That's all she wanted. Just to be left alone.

"How'd it go this morning?" Mother called eagerly (too eagerly to be natural, JoBeth decided) from the kitchen. She was fixing Sunday brunch, and part of it, JoBeth could tell from the delicious fragrance, would be blueberry waffles.

"Oh, it was okay. No big deal." It was probably best not to mention she'd tried to ride Rye or that some stranger had spoiled the whole morning.

Father came in from the music room with part of the Sunday paper under his arm. "I'm glad you went out, JoBeth," he said mildly. "It was certainly too nice a morning to waste indoors." His face was serene and composed; it was that scholar's look JoBeth admired so much and hoped to have herself someday. Seeing him so calm made it hard to remember he was the same person who'd betrayed her only two nights ago.

"By the way, JoBeth," he added with a familiar, absent-minded smile, "Robin's been calling you all morning. I gather she's got something cooking; she wants you to call her back as soon as you can." He smoothed her hair gently as he passed by on his way to the kitchen. JoBeth smothered a wild wish to grab onto her father's hand, to throw her arms around his neck. She'd never done anything like that in her life. To do so now would only embarrass them both.

After brunch, JoBeth dialed Robin's number from the phone in the upstairs hallway. Robin must've been sitting by the one at her end because it only rang once before JoBeth heard a delighted squeal: "Hey, Jo, I got this wonderful idea! I think it'd be neat if you . . ."

"Rob, I don't feel like . . ." JoBeth tried to say, but Robin's words galloped over her own and would not be halted until JoBeth rested the phone back in its cradle. If only people would quit thinking up things for me to do, JoBeth thought wearily.

When she showered before bedtime, JoBeth scrubbed and shampooed extra well to make sure she erased the last faint smell of horse. She realized belatedly that going to the club had been a mistake. Nothing healing had happened out there that would help her to forget Ashleigh and get on with her own life. As soon as her hair was dry, JoBeth pulled on the old, soft nightgown that ought to be thrown away. She stopped a moment at Ashleigh's bedroom on her way back to her own.

A Raggedy Ann doll languished against Ashleigh's pink pillow bolster. JoBeth imagined that its shoe-button eyes beckoned to her. She tiptoed into the room, pulled back the covers of her sister's bed, slipped into it. She would only stay a minute. She reached out to take the doll's hand in her own. It was friendly and forgiving.

JoBeth closed her eyes. Next to the museum, the private world inside her own skull was the one she liked best. Her thoughts began to wander. Why had that boy at the club seemed so familiar? Ah, of course . . . he reminded her of that boy in the photograph in *The Past and People of Ancient Luristan.* . . . Was Ashleigh's bed softer than her own? . . . Maybe so, because suddenly she felt so sleepy.

JoBeth stretched and sighed. Only a few days ago she'd felt pleased and happy to touch the cool, safe exterior of the stone pony. But when she began to dream, JoBeth felt the warm, satiny, cream-and-oatmeal hide of a horse named Rye beneath her fingertips.

5

Voices nibbled rudely at the edges of JoBeth's sleep. She tried to push them away, hated their sharp teeth, the way they tried to rouse her. If only she never had to wake up again, could hide forever in soothing darkness. But one voice, shriller and more anxious than the other one, dragged her to the surface of wakefulness.

"It's been a lot harder for her than we thought it might be," the voice lamented. JoBeth opened her eyes and stared at the ceiling. For months and weeks, *her* had meant only one person. Ashleigh. Now someone was talking about the other her. Herself.

"Michael, when I went to wake her just now, she wasn't in her own bed."

"Not in her own bed?" Her father's voice was calm, not yet concerned. Of course, it was a scholar's way not to go leaping to conclusions. "Then where . . ."

"She's sleeping in Ashleigh's bed, Michael. Holding onto that old Raggedy Ann doll my mother made as if her life depended on it."

JoBeth blinked. She looked at the walls of the room, the curtains, the bedspread. They *were* pink, not blue as her own would be! Raggedy Ann's soft hand was still buried in her own. (But she'd only intended to rest for a minute, just to see what it felt like to be Ashleigh.) JoBeth slid out of bed, padded to the top of the stairs, and looked down. Below, through the kitchen door that stood slightly ajar, she could see her parents leaning earnestly toward one another over the steam from their coffee cups.

"Mag Malowan has spoken to me about it, too, Michael. She said JoBeth sometimes makes inappropriate remarks like, 'What's the best way to lock death up?' or 'Should I file it under *D*?" *No, no,* JoBeth wanted to call down the stairs, *I never meant to really say those things, only to think them!*

"And Mag says JoBeth carries a little notebook with her all the time, scribbles strange things in it out of old books at the museum, always wants to be alone. Robin called me, too, Michael. She says JoBeth won't even talk to her anymore."

"Carol, all of us need time to get over what's happened this summer," JoBeth heard her father say. Thank heavens for his refusal to get all excited. "A death in any family is a terrible dislocation. It takes time to get adjusted. We're all upset—Mag Malowan included. Why, I think even Munchie feels the difference in our lives. Let's try not to make mountains out of molehills, Carol."

There. That ought to take care of that.

But JoBeth heard her mother go on insistently: "Michael, this is a problem we can't afford to ignore." Now her voice was shrill with conviction. "You and I both know that JoBeth's always been especially shy and sensitive—maybe even a lonely child. What happened to Ashleigh has only made it all worse. Maybe it was natural for JoBeth to be jealous of her sister. But just because Ashleigh is gone doesn't mean that JoBeth's problem has gone away, too."

It's a lie! JoBeth wanted to protest. *I wasn't ever jealous of Ashleigh!* "I had lots and lots of things Ashleigh never had," she could've explained if they'd given her a chance. "I am composed, and I have marvelous manners, and my handwriting is just like my father's, and in case you don't know it I'm going to decode some symbols that're carved on the stomach of the stone pony, so I don't see how anybody can say I was jealous of my sister."

"Perhaps we should encourage JoBeth to talk to Dr. Ryan," her father sighed. JoBeth watched him run a hand wearily through his silver hair. She digested his suggestion. Well, Dr. Ryan was pink and white and always smelled as fresh as a powdered baby. If she had to talk to him just to keep peace in the family, JoBeth guessed she could stand it.

"Dr. Ryan is a minister, Michael. He's not a psychiatrist."

A *psychiatrist* . . .? "Then you think JoBeth needs to see someone for professional counseling?"

"Yes, I do, Michael. And soon."

JoBeth padded softly back to Ashleigh's room. She felt the same way she had that evening she decided to lie in Queen Victoria's linen chest. She was growing smaller and smaller; her bones were dissolving in her limbs; there was a hole in her chest where her heart was supposed to be. She leaned over Ashleigh's bed, smoothed the bedcovers (she'd slept so soundly they were hardly wrinkled at all) and settled Raggedy Ann in place against the pink bolster.

In her own room, JoBeth pulled off her nightgown and dropped it into the wastebasket at the corner of her desk. The body she caught sight of in the mirror on the closet door was hardly more than a child's body, thin and straight-legged, its breasts small, its hips innocent of any rounded, girlish flesh. Such a body was an embarrassment. In gym class, when everybody else undressed for the showers, JoBeth could see that other girls looked like girls were supposed to look, not like little kids. She was the only one who was different.

Different.

She'd always tried to avoid thinking about that. Just like she avoided wondering why Ashleigh had been born tall and golden and she got to be the one who was skinny and freckled.

And now my parents think I'm crazy, too, she thought. JoBeth touched the rough spots on her forehead. In another week the skin would be smooth again. "How will I ever get the nerve to tell Robin I have to start seeing a shrink if I never could tell her about being glad Ashleigh doesn't have to wear handcuffs anymore?" she wondered out loud.

JoBeth went back to the top of the stairs. She could hear her mother dial the phone downstairs and begin to talk urgently to someone at the other end of the line.

The Medical Arts Building was in the center of the city, not far from the public library. "I'll check out some books and wait for you at the library," Mother said, squeezing JoBeth's fingers. "Afterward we can run over to Donelson's for a soda."

JoBeth retrieved her fingers. "I think I'd rather go alone if you don't mind."

"Alone?" Her mother hugged her as if she were anxious to undo some past neglect. She's practically forty-five years old, JoBeth thought. Other kids had mothers who looked their age. The body pressed against her own was the long, lean body of an expert tennis player, not like anybody's mother ought to be.

JoBeth twisted out of her mother's embrace as politely as she could. "Do you have any bus tokens?" she asked. "I'd better get going or I'll be late for that appointment." When JoBeth left the house, she didn't look back but knew that if she had, she would see her mother standing at the front window, a hand pressed against her lips.

Dr. Morris's secretary had red hair and a very dark suntan. Her glasses were the smoky kind that turned smokier in sunlight and had a tiny gold butterfly in the corner of the left lens.

"Please be seated, Miss Cunningham," she said in a soothing voice, "Dr. Morris will be with you in a moment." That's all it was, too, only a moment until Dr. Morris opened the door of his office and a middle-aged woman who looked as if she'd been crying all afternoon stepped out. Dr. Morris beckoned JoBeth inside.

If he takes one patient right after the other all day long, JoBeth wondered, how does he ever get time to go to the bathroom? But maybe that's what Mother and Miss Malowan meant by having inappropriate thoughts. JoBeth straightened her shoulders, folowed Dr. Morris, and promised herself that she would have only the appropriate kind.

The inside of the doctor's office was just as soothing as his receptionist's voice. The walls were papered in a genteel beige-and-brown pattern that looked like a bamboo forest. The draperies were the color of oyster shells and diffused the light in a pleasing way. All the diplomas on the wall behind the doctor's desk looked alike. It was the sort of room that might tempt a person to forget why she'd been sent there. JoBeth made up her mind not to be easily tricked.

Dr. Morris held out his hand. JoBeth stuck hers into it and let him shake it. He made her feel like Charlie had, like she was trying to grow up but hadn't made it yet. "Sit down, JoBeth," he invited. "Why don't you tell me a little bit about yourself."

JoBeth was surprised. "Didn't my mother tell you why she wanted me to come here?"

"Yes, JoBeth, your mother did tell me a few things. Now I'd like to hear from you."

"My sister—her name was Ashleigh and she was four years older than me—she died from a bite by the fourth sign of the zodiac."

Dr. Morris was about to make a note on the yellow pad he held on his knee but arrested his pen in midair. "A bite from the fourth sign of the zodiac? I don't quite understand, JoBeth. I thought your mother told me that . . ."

"The fourth sign of the zodiac is the water sign. You know—the crab. It's called the sign of cancer, too."

"Ah. Of course. You mention the zodiac, JoBeth. Are you interested in such things? I mean, magic and tarot cards and witchcraft? Those sorts of things?"

"Not really." Why should she be? That stuff was for

superstitious types, not for scholars. "See, Dr. Morris, in Greek legend the only bad thing the crab ever did was pinch Heracles when he battled the Hydra," JoBeth explained. "Except I don't think the Greeks knew how bad the crab—cancer, I mean—was going to turn out to be."

Then it was his turn. JoBeth waited for him to say something. Dr. Morris studied her silently. JoBeth wished she hadn't mentioned the zodiac. Maybe it made her sound really crazy.

Finally, probing the way you learn to probe an amoeba in biology class to make it wiggle under the microscope, Dr. Morris asked, "And how did you feel about that, JoBeth? About your sister's death?"

"Glad. I guess I felt glad."

"Glad?"

"Yes. See, it was a terrible thing for Ashleigh. On account of she was the kind of person who loved the outdoors and the sun and swimming and that stuff. Nothing like cancer should've happened to my sister. At first, I thought maybe cancer'd be like whenever they show it on TV. People only have to be sick a little while; then they look sleepy and die just before the commercial. But it isn't that way in real life. Our whole family was sick. Even our dog Munchie doesn't feel good anymore."

"Have you ever wished it'd been you who died, JoBeth?"

"Never," she lied quickly. Too quickly? She didn't like the careful attention Dr. Morris was paying to everything she said.

"Are you angry with Ashleigh for dying, JoBeth?"

"Of course not. That'd be dumb. It wasn't her fault. She didn't want to die. She wanted to ride horseback and play tennis and go bike riding with her boyfriends forever."

"That seems quite natural, doesn't it, JoBeth? It might be what most young girls want. Maybe it's what you'd like to do, too."

"Oh, I'm different," JoBeth explained. "See, I'm not like that." She was surprised he hadn't been able to see that right away. "I'm going to be the director of a famous museum someday, just like my father. I won't have time for the stuff Ashleigh liked. Someday I'll have a house of my own with books on shelves that go from the floor to the ceiling. Some of those books I'll even write myself. No, I'm not at all like my sister. We were as different as night and day."

"Well, JoBeth, maybe not as different as you might like to think. You see, all of us want to be loved and to be able to love back. Of course, to love means to take a risk, for what we love we might someday lose." Dr. Morris paused. "And sometimes, JoBeth, adolescence can pose other problems for those of us who are especially sensitive." His voice sounded a lot like his wallpaper looked. "We are challenged to grow up, you see. Our bodies change; sex can become a disturbing factor in our lives, too. In other words, JoBeth, life can all of a sudden get complicated for us—even when there's been nothing as dramatic as a death in the family for us to cope with."

Sex. The word always annoyed JoBeth. X was a dumb letter; who invented it in the first place? Probably not the Sumerians; five thousand years ago people must've had better sense. The thing about *x* was, it held its arms high over its head like it was shouting.

"I like the museum best when it's empty," JoBeth said. It was time to change the subject. "It's quiet then, which makes it easier to work on decoding those letters on the stomach of the stone pony."

"How do you feel when you're alone at the museum, JoBeth?" Dr. Morris asked, ignoring the subject of the stone pony.

"Alone." How'd he think she felt? Being a psychiatrist must get boring; it made you ask some pretty weird questions. JoBeth realized she was bored, too. Her thoughts began to wander. The image of the stone pony floated through her mind .... Had Father's hair still been partly brown when he tried to pick Mintaka, Alnitam, and Alnitah out of Orion's belt? ... She'd been surprised that Rye's coat was so sleek, just like satin. JoBeth allowed herself a quick peek at Dr. Morris. His eyebrows were thick and black; it was impossible to tell if his eyes were kind or cruel.

"Have you ever taken any drugs, JoBeth?" he asked unexpectedly. He smiled, as if to let her know the question did not necessarily imply criticism. "Smoked any marijuana, for instance?"

JoBeth stared at him. "Marijuana?" she echoed. So being glad Ashleigh was relieved of her pain, trying to decode some writing that'd been carved into a clay horse—he thought such things were due to marijuana? JoBeth was glad she hadn't made the mistake of telling him about Queen Victoria's linen chest. Or that an exercise boy at the Ohio Hunt and Show Club looked exactly like a boy in a hundred-year-old book about Luristan.

JoBeth studied her watch and her freckles. "I have to go," she announced politely. Even crazy people could afford marvelous manners.

"Our hour isn't up yet, JoBeth."

"It is now." When she rushed through the reception room, JoBeth was sure she saw the gold butterfly on the left lens of the red-haired lady's glasses shut its wings in astonishment.

As soon as she left Dr. Morris's office, JoBeth hurried down the street to the library. It took twenty minutes to find exactly the book she wanted. "My goodness, this isn't your usual kind of reading matter, JoBeth," the librarian remarked with a smile. "*Grooming and Riding Your First Horse*—well, I can see you're planning a wonderful summer."

Taking charge of your own life. That's what Mrs. Dawson in Mental Hygiene class called it last year. "I'm about to take charge of my own life," JoBeth said. It sounded very effective. The librarian looked impressed, too.

JoBeth announced part of her decision at the dinner table. "I'm not going back to see that Dr. Morris," she began. From the looks on her parents' faces, it was plain the bad news about her unfinished hour of therapy had already floated down from the eleventh floor of the Medical Arts Building.

"Well, darling, let's try not to worry about that right now," Mother said. "Try to enjoy your meal; maybe we can all talk about it later." She must've played tennis all afternoon, JoBeth thought; she was even darker than Dr. Morris's secretary.

Ordinarily, it was one of JoBeth's favorite suppers—teriyaki chicken with fried rice. "I know I'm going to feel a lot better by the end of the summer," she said. She wanted to make them feel better. She racked her brain for the exact words Father had used yesterday.

"A death in the family is a terrible dislocation. We shouldn't make mountains out of molehills. It just takes time to get adjusted, that's all." Wasn't it strange how people talked about time? Take time . . . find time . . . buy time . . . kill time. JoBeth carved a four lane highway on the yellow tablecloth with the tines of her fork.

"Has either of you ever wondered if I smoked marijuana?"

Her mother seemed to blanch under her tan. When Father raised his coffee cup to his lips, JoBeth could see that his hand trembled. There were tired shadows under his eyes, too, along with hollow places in his cheeks that JoBeth had never noticed before. Just the same, he answered calmly and patiently, "No, I don't believe we ever have, JoBeth."

"Well—I thought about it. Robin got some once. From a friend of Charlie's." She studied her plate. She hadn't smoked any of it because number one, she didn't know how to smoke and number two, she'd been afraid to.

That was the story of her life, wasn't it? She was afraid of so many things. Horses. The dumb letter *x*. Boys who grew up to wear beards that covered up dimples. On top of it all, her teriyaki sauce was leaking into her fried rice.

JoBeth laid her fork aside. "I'll finish my supper later, okay? I don't feel so hot right now. Maybe I'll go upstairs and lie down for a little while."

The window in her room was open; its soft blue curtain stirred in the breeze. JoBeth trailed her fingers along the sill and watched Mrs. Dalrymple back her new car out of the garage next door. The car was blue, too.

JoBeth thought about the boy in the blue shirt. The wave he'd given her the other day seemed shy. Timid, even. Maybe he was a lot like she was herself. Didn't seem all that much older, either. JoBeth stopped running her fingers across the smooth sill.

On the other hand, he must know *something* about taking charge of life. After all, he had a real job. Exercising horses at a big, well-known stable like the Ohio Hunt and Show Club had to be pretty demanding. JoBeth glanced at her desk where she'd tossed the library book she hadn't read yet.

What if Ashleigh was right? she thought. Maybe I have spent too much time thinking about the past. *Let it go, Joey.* Ashleigh'd said that, too. JoBeth sat down and began to leaf through the library book. Maybe it was time to find out if there was another JoBeth Cunningham out there somewhere.

6

"Good morning, JoBeth!" Mrs. Wilson called merrily through the office window. Confronted by Mrs. Wilson's wide, ordinary face it was hard not to feel sane and sensible, too. "This is the second time in a week you've been out to see us," Mrs. Wilson exclaimed. "Does that mean you've decided to keep your sister's horse after all?"

Mrs. Wilson was a conclusion-leaper, like Mother. "I guess we haven't actually decided anything for sure," JoBeth hedged. "Coming out here is just something for me to do until we make up our minds. Maybe we'll run an ad for Rye in the paper next week."

It was her own idea; it was a way to keep from getting too committed to a project that might not have any future anyway. "I don't expect it'll take long to get rid of him once we begin advertising. He's a nice horse—as horses go." *Get rid of him.* JoBeth wished she hadn't expressed it quite that way.

"Well, dear, the club will be busy for the next several weeks, and you might even find a buyer for Rye among our own membership. We'll be putting on a Benefit again—it's our sixth annual, you know—and life won't be as quiet around here as it's seemed recently."

"A Benefit?"

"Your sister won a blue ribbon at our fourth, don't you remember?" JoBeth nodded, pretending she did. Maybe it was the one framed and hanging next to that newspaper clipping in the music room. "The proceeds from the Benefit go to St. Benedict's Hospital. As I recall, JoBeth, your father is on their board of directors."

"Guess I don't pay much attention to that kind of stuff," JoBeth admitted. "But I promise I won't get in anybody's way while you're getting ready for the show. Anyway, Rye'll probably be sold by that time."

"Ever thought about entering the Benefit yourself, JoBeth? We have many different classes; one doesn't have to be a professional horseperson, and there'll be classes for beginners, too."

"Oh, I don't think . . . remember, Mrs. Wilson, I told you I'm not exactly into horses. Not this kind, I mean. There's a stone po—"

"Perhaps what you need is a smaller horse, JoBeth."

Yes, JoBeth thought, one about three inches tall. "No, you see, there's a stone pony in our Luristan diorama at the museum. That's the kind of horse I meant. The symbolic kind." But that isn't quite true, is it, JoBeth? a small voice chided her. You may indeed have your cuneiform notebook in your hip pocket— but you've got a library book about real horses in your knapsack! All of which was confusing to *her*, so how could it be explained to Mrs. Wilson? Luckily, Mrs.

Wilson made it easy not to have to. "Well, each to her own, dear; that's what I always say!"

JoBeth collected her tack from the tack room before she stopped to check on Rye. If she hurried, maybe she could get him brushed and saddled and be out on one of the bridle paths before anyone paid much attention to her. When she arrived at Rye's stall, he whinnied softly and bobbed his smoky head at her. He's just like Munchie, JoBeth thought, so eager to see a person. Maybe it was one of the reasons Ashleigh had liked animals so well.

"Hi, goofy horse," JoBeth whispered, suspecting she was the goofy one. "I think maybe you're beginning to like me a little." Rye bobbed his head again as if to say, *Yes, yes; I do!*

JoBeth clipped her lead rope onto the ring on his halter and led him into the wide aisle of the barn. She fastened the rope to a hitch ring that was bolted into the front of the stall. She propped her book from the library up on the shelf formed where the wood partition of the stall met the wire screen. What if that boy in the blue shirt didn't work today? JoBeth pushed the possibility out of her mind.

" 'Use the curry comb with a light, circular motion,' " she read out loud. " 'Its primary purpose is to break up dried sweat and matted hair.' " She studied Rye. Hardly any of his hair looked matted. Of course, he hadn't been ridden in several weeks. " '*Never* use the curry comb below the knee on the foreleg of your horse or below the hock on his hindleg, as the bone lies close to the surface in these areas and is especially sensitive to bruising.' "

JoBeth worked steadily until she developed a

rhythm for the proper light, circular motion. Thoughts of boys in blue shirts faded from her mind, so she was startled to have a voice behind her suggest mildly: "Ma'am, excuse me. The safest way to tie your horse when you groom him in a barn is to cross-tie him. Here, let me show you how."

JoBeth turned. Well, at least his eyes weren't two empty black holes. They were gray eyes, shaded by straight, sooty lashes. Although he'd seemed small before, JoBeth could now see that he was a full head taller than she was. He was still wearing the blue shirt she'd seen him in several days ago. It was deeply soiled around the neck, and half-moons of sweat-stain darkened the underarms. His boots, which might once have been good yellow cowhide, were runover and worn.

"Cross-tie him?" she repeated blankly. She could feel blood rush upward from her chest to color her neck and turn her cheeks red.

"Sure. Look, this is how to do it." The boy unsnapped the tie, ran it halfway through the halter ring, and knotted it so that the two ends were equal. Each end had a snap catch, one of which he fastened on the left side of the aisle, the other on the right side. "Now nobody has to walk right behind your horse, ma'am; he gets passed on the side, see? Makes for a safe barn. But then, you're the lucky kind anyhow."

"Lucky?" JoBeth felt stupid; all she was doing was echoing everything he said.

"To have a horse of your own and all that." The boy's voice had a soft, slurred accent that JoBeth was sure had originated in some state far south of Ohio. "All *I* do is ride other folks' horses. Like ol' High Pockets here." He nodded toward the horse he held by its bridle, the same tall bay horse with four white socks and blazed face he'd been riding that first day. The boy grinned and ran his fingers through his own dark, lank hair. He wasn't especially good-looking, JoBeth decided, but at least he didn't wear a beard.

"I'm not as lucky as you think," she explained uneasily. Mrs. Wilson had said he was a new employee of the club. He probably didn't know anything about Ashleigh. "See, this isn't actually my horse."

"Whose is it, then?"

"My sister's." JoBeth clamped her lips over her braces and kept her voice cool. He didn't act as timid as she'd hoped he would. She turned her back and went back to brushing Rye.

After a moment the boy teased gently: "Huh! Guess I better look for friendlier company in one of the other barns."

"If company's what you're looking for, it'd probably be a good idea," JoBeth agreed. "I came out here to be alone," she lied, "to be alone and do some heavy thinking." Two days ago, she'd hoped they might have something in common. Up close, he seemed as different from her as Ashleigh had been.

The boy tapped the end of his horse's reins lightly against his flexed knee. "No harm to thinking, that's for sure. A bum like me probably oughta try it more often." JoBeth kept her back to him. It was hard not to be curious, though. "Are you really? A bum, I mean?" No wonder he'd seemed different.

The boy laughed. JoBeth brushed down to Rye's knees and peeked up under her arm. The boy's teeth were very white and somewhat crooked, and his smile had an offbeat kind of charm.

"Naw. Not exactly. Right now I'm a gopher. You

know—go fer that horse, Luke. Luke, go fer some hay. That kind of gopher."

"Is that your name—Luke?"

"Yes, ma'am, it is. What's yours?"

"JoBeth." Except for Dr. Morris, she hadn't held as long a conversation with anyone in more than four weeks. So why choose a person like this? JoBeth continued to brush Rye and considered in her mind's eye the boy's dirty boots, his soiled shirt, his heavy black hair. She imagined if she moved any closer, he might smell unsavory, too. Nevertheless, she heard herself inquire politely: "You go to school around here, Luke?"

"School?" He snorted. "Not likely! I dropped outa that scene a long time back."

That did it. If he didn't go to school, he probably didn't read much either. Wouldn't know how to play chess. Would think Luristan was a new kind of pizza. JoBeth resolutely kept her back turned.

But he was slow to take the hint. "What do you do when you aren't grooming this horse for your sister, JoBeth?" he persisted.

"I have a job," JoBeth answered airily, "which is where I have to go the minute I get through here." There was no need to explain it was a make-do kind of job, that her salary came from her father's own pocket and not from museum funds. From the corner of her eye, JoBeth saw Luke slide a glance at the brass nameplate on the door of Rye's stall.

"Well, I reckon I'll just wait around till that ol' Ashleigh Susan shows up!" he declared with forced cheer. "Ain't no way she can be as disagreeable as you!"

JoBeth stopped her curry comb in mid-stroke.

"You might have a long wait. My sister died four weeks ago." She realized, with a twinge of shame, that she had wanted to say those words.

"Hey. Wow." Luke seemed more stricken than any stranger ought to have been. "Listen, I didn't aim to make you feel bad or make you talk if you didn't want to. But when I saw you the other day, I thought to myself, 'Luke, there's somebody who—' But, hey—I'm sorry. It ain't none of my business anyhow." With that, Luke turned on his heel and led High Pockets out of the barn. He didn't look back.

JoBeth watched him go with a hollow feeling in the pit of her stomach. It'd always been so easy for her to do: to turn aside a friendly gesture. She didn't want to be that way, but it was a push-pull sort of thing: she often wanted to pull close to someone, only to find herself pushing that person away. She'd done it with Ralph Smith's aunt . . . and Robin . . . and Charlie . . . not to mention Dr. Morris.

But this time, as she watched the boy named Luke walk away, shoulders high and thin and sharp under his dirty blue shirt, JoBeth wished she hadn't needed to do it again.

7

"I'm ready to leave, JoBeth," Miss Malowan called from the hallway. "If you hurry, I can drop you off at your house on my way downtown. I'm sure we can make it before the storm gets worse."

JoBeth touched her forehead. It was smooth again. "Thanks, Miss Malowan," she called back, "but I've already got a ride."

Okay, JoBeth, she muttered to herself, think up another fib to make this one more convincing. "Charlie's coming by to pick me up in about ten minutes," she added. "We're going over to his house to play chess and drink root beer." Miss Malowan liked to play chess herself; it was a fib bound to please her.

"Wonderful, JoBeth!" Miss Malowan poked her head into the office, beamed, and headed toward the front entrance with a vigorous "See you tomorrow!" thrown back over one shoulder.

It was only a summer squall anyway, JoBeth thought, nothing to get alarmed about. She flicked through *The Past and People of Ancient Luristan* before reaching for the key to the diorama case. She found the photograph of the boy who reminded her of Luke. How disappointing; the two boys didn't resemble one another at all. To imagine they had was only another chance to feel more comfortable with the past than the present. JoBeth snapped the book shut. She'd have to think about *that* later; with Miss Malowan gone for the night, there were more important things to do.

JoBeth ran downstairs, unlocked the Luristan diorama, and picked the stone horse out of his meadow. She spread a paper tissue flat on one of the glass cases in the middle of the room where the light was brightest. She turned the pony on his side. Just because that crazy notion of taking care of Ashleigh's horse—riding it, even—hadn't turned out too well, it didn't mean she ought to give up her scheme to decipher the script on the clay horse.

Father said that many famous archeological discoveries had been made by people who had the courage to follow hunches. That's what JoBeth decided she had: a hunch. She liked to think it was like the one Heinrich Schliemann had that led him to the discovery of the buried city of Troy.

Schliemann, who was German, was only seven years old in 1829 when *his* father showed him a picture of the Greek city of Troy in flames. Schliemann grew up to become a wealthy businessman, but the image of Troy haunted him. Finally, he began to read about the ruined city; he dreamed of Troy; at last, he went in search of it.

For centuries scholars had claimed that, according to Greek legends, the city must be located near Bunarbashi. But after studying many maps of ancient trade routes, Schliemann concluded it lay to the north, beneath the sands of Hisarlik. His logic was derided by Greek scholars. Schliemann replied that history should not be bent to suit the wishes of scholars; rather it should be based on scientific inquiry. At last, working with only the help of his young Greek wife, Schliemann did indeed uncover the fabled city of Troy, something no one else had ever been able to do.

If a hunch worked for him, maybe mine will work for me, JoBeth told herself. Hers was really quite simple and was based on her father's own words. If Father had stood on a mountain peak in Luristan and said to himself: "I'm so near to heaven I can pick the stars out of Orion's belt," then why might not one of the lost horsemen have imagined exactly the same thing thousands of years before? And if one had, might he not also have decided to make a tribute to Orion, the god of the hunt, by carving Orion's name into the underside of a small clay pony?

A peal of thunder shuddered over the Archer. JoBeth glanced toward the glass doors that faced the garden. The coming storm made it darker outside than it usually would be by eight-thirty. But it hadn't started to rain hard yet; only a few occasional drops dampened the courtyard with black spots as big as quarters. JoBeth turned back to her job.

She wadded up a second tissue. She propped the pony's feet in the air so that the lights overhead focused directly on the writing inscribed on his underside. Lightning illuminated the garden again.

The rain started to drum on the glass doors and interfered with JoBeth's concentration. She looked outside again. The stones of the courtyard were covered with water. Thunder sounded once more. The lights over her head flickered once, twice, like candles in the wind, then went out altogether.

"Just what you needed, Heinrich," she groaned. "A power failure. . . ." Fortunately, such outages never lasted long; the lights would be back on again in a minute or two. Mother and Father would be worried, though; maybe she ought to call them. No, the phones were probably out of order, too. Worse, there wasn't enough light left in the room to see clearly either the stone pony's stomach or the pages of her notebook.

JoBeth gathered up the edges of the tissue and cradled the stone poney to her chest. She walked to the glass doors and peered outside. The stuff Miss Malowan called bougainvillea hung like witch's hair from the stone wall of the building. Red petals stripped from the potted geraniums swirled like drops of blood in the black rainwater. The nymph in the fountain was the only thing that still looked happy. She held a marble hand aloft and smiled cheerfully through the storm.

It was several seconds before JoBeth would admit to herself that the nymph was not alone in the garden.

Someone, a suspiciously dark and dirty someone, was feeling his way hand-over-hand around the rim of the nymph's fountain. The rain had pasted his soiled blue shirt to his thin body. In another moment he was rapping urgently on the glass only an inch from her nose.

JoBeth didn't take time to decide what was the best thing to do. She slid the door open and Luke jumped inside.

"What are *you* doing here?" she demanded. She didn't know if she should be scared or angry.

Luke stood, shivering and hunch-shouldered, in a pool of rainwater. "Lordy, didn't I have the devil's own time finding this place," he gasped. "I'd have been here long before that storm broke, but I sorta lost my way and . . ." His voice might've been southern and soft, JoBeth realized, but there was a peculiar secretiveness in his eyes that made her feel ill at ease.

"How'd you know where to find me?"

"You said you had a job, remember?" Luke shook himself like a wet dog and sprinkled water generously in a dozen different directions. The cleaning men would have extra work tonight, JoBeth could see. "I just asked Mrs. Wilson where you worked. It was simple."

Luke shifted his weight from one wet foot to the other. JoBeth hoped he was sorry he'd come. He glanced at her hands folded around the stone pony. "What's that you got there?" he asked politely. Just like at the club this afternoon, he seemed anxious to breathe life into their conversation.

JoBeth held the pony out and pulled back an edge of its tissue blanket. There'd been so much she wanted to accomplish tonight! "It's an artifact," she said.

"Funny, I'd swear it looks almost like a horse."

"Of course it's a horse," JoBeth said testily. She didn't feel like a person with marvelous manners anymore. "A three-thousand-year-old horse from the province of Luristan, if you want to get particular about it. Which also means it's an artifact—or to use the archeological definition, 'a product of primitive human workmanship.'"

"Me and archeology are not acquainted, but me and horses are old buddies. Can I have a look at him?"

JoBeth reluctantly passed the stone pony to him.

77

"Be careful," she warned. "He's part of our permanent collection. Actually, I shouldn't even have him out of the glass case he belongs in."

Luke turned the stone pony over and over in his hands. The manner in which he handled the clay horse made her think of her father: it was careful and interested and respectful.

"Nice little fella, ain't he?" Luke mused. "Makes me think of a Morgan, that's what. Carries his head high up and proud; got short cannon bones, too, and sloping pasterns," he pointed out. JoBeth had no idea what in the world he was talking about. "That ol' Justin Morgan was some horse: part Arab and part Barb, or so some folks claim. Did heavy farm work all his life, that horse did, or cleared woodlots out there in Vermont—but today you'll find his kin in fancy show rings all around the country." He passed the stone horse back to her.

"Really?" JoBeth said drily.

"By the way, what're those gouges in his belly?"

"Those gouges, as you call them, are an ancient form of writing called cuneiform script." Now *she* would tell *him* a thing or two. "None of us here at the museum know for sure exactly what they mean. Not yet. That's what I was working on when the lights went out—trying to decipher that script."

"No kidding." Somehow she'd expected him to be more impressed. On the contrary, he made an observation that startled her: "You ever noticed that statue's almost the same color as your sister's horse? Some folks call that color buckskin. Others call it dun. That color horse usually has a dorsal stripe, too."

"Is that the mark that goes all the way down Rye's back and kind of blends into his tail?"

"Yep, that's a dorsal stripe all right." Luke peered around the dimly-lit Lower Level. JoBeth followed his glance with her own. How impressive everything looked: dioramas and displays of brass and ivory and jade. Except that apparently was not quite what Luke saw.

"This is a real weird place," he said softly. "Ever noticed there's no noise in here? No smell, either? It's sort of, what's that word, petrified." Static, frozen, dead, in other words. There was no end to his insolence. "You like working in a place like this?" he chirped. It was clearly the most farfetched thing he'd ever heard of.

"Of course I like it," JoBeth snapped. He was beginning to get on her nerves. "Why shouldn't I? My father's been the director of the Archer for more than twenty years. Someday I'll probably run a place just like this myself."

"That ain't what you ought to be doing right now, though."

JoBeth felt like screaming. Just what she needed: one more person who knew what was good for her. "And I suppose *you* have a better idea?" she asked tartly.

"Yeah. That's why I asked Mrs. Wilson where you worked. I wanted to tell you that . . . well, that you ought to be out in the sunshine learning how to ride that little yellow horse of your sister's."

JoBeth stared at him. He stared back, and seemed almost as amazed by his words as she was. "Then maybe you could even be in that Benefit show Mrs. Wilson told me about."

"What would that prove?"

"That you could. Ain't that enough?"

JoBeth hugged the stone pony a little tighter. "I went to a girls camp in Colorado once," she admitted. "It was called Bide-A-While. They were supposed to teach people how to ride, too. I didn't learn anything. Only how to fall off."

The lights overhead flickered and came on. Deep in the bowels of the Archer the air conditioning system began to hum again. JoBeth was almost sorry. In another moment she might have agreed to . . .

"Well, guess I gotta get going," Luke said, as if he too understood that a spell had been broken. He opened the glass doors. The rain had stopped, and the air was fragrant with the smell of bougainvillea. He paused and turned back. JoBeth realized suddenly why the secretive look in his eyes bothered her; it was the same one she'd seen every night in her own when she leaned close to the diorama case.

"The offer still stands," Luke called softly. "If you wanta learn to ride your sister's horse, I can teach you how." Then he was gone.

8

If you wanta learn to ride your sister's horse, I can teach you how. . . .

When JoBeth woke in the morning, she knew she would take Luke up on his offer. Not that it was the way she'd intended to spend the summer. All I planned to do was decipher that script on the stone pony, she mused as she pulled her clothes on. Father had said he'd do it himself when he had time; if she did it for him it would be like giving him a gift. Lately, though, JoBeth wondered if she might not be doing it for herself, not for him at all.

And the script itself? Well, it's waited a few thousand years, she thought. I guess it can wait for a few more weeks until I've had some riding lessons. Amazing. She'd never imagined putting a project that had anything to do with the museum on a back burner. The museum had always come first in her plans. Maybe the funeral had changed that, too, along with the importance of freckles and pronouns.

Breaking the news about riding lessons to Mother

81

and Father might be awkward, though. Especially since they believe I'm getting so weird I need to see a shrink, JoBeth thought as she hurried downstairs to the kitchen. She mulled over a dozen ways to tell them, each more complicated than the one before it. Then she decided to take charge of the news, just like she intended to take charge of her life.

"I know I've never been much for sports or out-doors stuff," she announced over breakfast, "but if it's okay with you guys, I'd like to take some riding lessons this summer." Mrs. Dawson might've given her an *A* for that. JoBeth was glad Mother had used the good blue breakfast plates; they looked just like she hoped her words sounded—healthy and optimistic. JoBeth was aware, even with lowered lashes, however, that her parents exchanged what old-fashioned novels called significant glances.

"Why, if you want to take some riding lessons," her mother said slowly, "I . . . we think that would be wonderful."

JoBeth knew her mother wanted to make the decision sound ordinary. Both of us know it isn't ordinary at all, she thought. She knows as well as I do that I can't tell my left foot from my right when it comes to anything athletic. JoBeth was tempted to reach across the table and give her mother's strong brown fingers a squeeze to let her know the pretense was appreciated. She kept her hands on her silverware. Warm, impulsive gestures that came so easily to other people always made her feel klutzy.

JoBeth cleared her throat. They'd want answers to other questions, of course. "There's a fellow at the club who can give me lessons," she volunteered before they asked. She darted a glance at her father. The blue shadows under his eyes told JoBeth that he still was not sleeping well. Maybe if she let him know how much good riding lessons would do her, it might help.

"I think getting out in the sun, getting some exercise and all that, maybe it'd be good therapy." Oops. JoBeth wished she could retrieve that word therapy. It would make Mother believe a return visit to the Medical Arts Building was a possibility.

"Speaking of therapy, JoBeth, I hope you've decided to . . ."

Wouldn't you know? JoBeth held up five warning fingers. "Only riding lessons right now, Mother. Afterwards, maybe I won't even need Dr. Morris." The morning sun glinted off the rim of JoBeth's blue plate. She scraped up a final mouthful of scrambled egg on a wedge of toast. "I'll get going so I can get home in time to clean up before getting down to the Archer." She got up, pushed her chair back in its place. There was still one other thing.

"Mrs. Wilson told me Ashleigh won a ribbon at some horse show at the club. Funny; I can't remember that."

JoBeth watched her father take a swallow of coffee. She'd always thought his silver hair was so distinguished. This morning he looked merely worn and aged. When he spoke, he stared through the window that overlooked the backyard and avoided her glance. "You didn't go with us that afternoon, JoBeth," he reminded her. "You said the club was too hot and you didn't care for all the flies and smells and confusion."

Now JoBeth remembered: Mother said since it was Ashleigh's first show, the whole family ought to be present. Flies and smells were the only excuses JoBeth could think of for not going that Sunday. Her real reason was much simpler. She'd made up her mind days before the Benefit not to watch Ashleigh win one more darn thing. Not one more blue ribbon, or another loving cup, or a different walnut plaque that would be set out on a shelf somewhere for the rest of the world to admire.

Luke was leading High Pockets out of a stall when JoBeth found him. She hooked her thumbs in her belt loops and tried to make her question sound like his answer didn't matter too much one way or the other. "Did you mean what you said last night?"

"Mean what?" The look that crept into his gray eyes was not exactly the one JoBeth expected to see there. It was the same fox-on-the-run expression she'd noticed the day she'd first glimpsed him through that screen of willow and alder leaves.

"You know. About helping me learn how to ride."

"Oh. That." Luke hiked one shoulder up and seemed relieved. "Sure, I meant it all right. Only I figured you'd decide you liked stone ponies better'n the real kind. You gonna enter the Benefit, too?"

"Oh, I don't think I could ever learn enough to . . . well, what *exactly* does a person have to do to be in it?"

"How old are you? That'll have something to do with it."

Should she fib a little and say she was fifteen? "I'm fourteen," JoBeth admitted.

"Then you'd be in a maiden class. Which don't mean you gotta be a girl. It means a junior entrant who's not eighteen yet and has never been in a show before." Luke scratched at his hair: It was the blackest hair JoBeth had ever seen, with highlights so deep they were almost purple.

"And if memory serves me right," Luke went on, "this here is zone five, same's we were in back home. Zone five takes in Indiana, Illinois, Michigan and Ohio, too—which means you'd have to meet the same requirements in competition that we had for our shows."

"Which are?"

"Seems to me the rule book said for a maiden class you had to know how to mount and dismount, back your horse, post to a trot, change diagonals on both a trot and canter, and . . ."

"Luke, I don't even know what those words mean! But I got a book from the library that tells how to . . ."

Luke dropped his chin to his collarbone and groaned. "Lady, do I have bad news for you! There's some things in this old world can't be learned by reading nice, polite words off a printed page. Some things in this world just gotta be *done!*" So he *had* gotten wind of Mrs. Dawson's take-charge philosophy.

Then Luke gave her a narrow gray glance. "Now, we got about six weeks before that Benefit takes place. If you have a two-hour lesson every day for six weeks, you *might* be able to do it. Can't make you no promises, though. It'd be awful hard work, too. And the only one who could really make it happen is *you,* JoBeth."

"Lessons every day for six weeks," JoBeth repeated, exhausted before she even started. "That won't give me time to do anything else. . . ." What would happen to research in hundred-year-old books with burgundy covers?

Luke noticed her hesitation. He touched her arm lightly. "Will it help any if I tell you I got a surefire method from Ol' Perce for teaching new riders? He called it his ASPSS Method." Labels, JoBeth mused. Everybody likes them.

"Who, may I ask, is Ol' Perce and what kind of . . ."

"The Application of the Seat of the Pants to the Seat of the Saddle," Luke explained with a grin, "and I ain't never seen it fail, either."

"Was Ol' Perce your riding teacher?" It seemed unlikely; if Luke didn't go to a regular school, would he be apt to go to riding school?

Luke grunted softly. "Naw. Ol' Perce was my uncle, my daddy's big brother." He finished cross-tying High Pockets and reached for a plastic bucket filled with grooming tools. "After my folks died, Ol' Perce and Miss Hattie took me in. They didn't have no young of their own, so it weren't much of a burden," He paused.

"Perce is gone now, though. Died more'n a year ago. But me and him had us some good times when he was alive! Yes, ma'am! Worked on some of the fanciest hunt and show clubs in the Bluegrass. Some of those stables sent horses and riders all over the country to compete in shows, sometimes even to places like Paris and London." His voice was warm with pride.

"Why'd you come up here to Ohio, then? Seems like you were so happy where you were."

Luke's smile faded. He took a hoof pick from the bucket. He placed his left hand on High Pockets' shoulder, ran his hand down the horse's foreleg to just above the fetlock. "Ever notice how things change sometimes, don't stay the way you'd like 'em to be?"

There's a lot I could tell him about that, JoBeth thought. She watched as Luke nudged High Pockets slightly, forcing the big bay to shift his weight. When he lifted the horse's hoof, it came up easily. Luke began to clean High Pockets' hoof with the pick by working expertly from heel to toe.

"Hardly any part of a horse is more important than his feet," he explained, "and if he gets thrush it could ruin him for good. Thrush, in case you don't know, is an infection a horse can get if he stands too long on wet, rotten bedding. The frog of his hoof—that's this raised, triangular part right here—gets all soft and spongy. And smell! If you've smelled it once, you won't likely forget it." A long, uneasy silence followed before Luke went on.

"See, Ol' Perce had the same failing my daddy did. Winters, he called the stuff cough medicine. Summers, it was his tonic. Miss Hattie told him she'd brew up some sulfur and molasses, but Perce allowed that wasn't the kinda tonic he had in mind." Luke worked the hoof pick under High Pockets' shoe. "I don't care what him or my daddy called it, though. It sure smelled like booze to me. Whatever it was, it fetched my daddy off the road one night; the wreck killed him, and my mama, too. Dying took Perce longer, though. What got him was sirocco of the liver."

JoBeth winced. "You mean cirrhosis of the liver, Luke. It's a disease people can get from drinking too much alcohol. A sirocco is a kind of wind that blows in places like Africa."

"Learned that outa some fancy book, I bet," Luke observed drily. He pried a stubborn gravel chip out of the corner of High Pockets' shoe. "I didn't set out to tell you my whole life story, JoBeth. But when you told me your sister'd died, well, I sorta knew just how you felt."

To be understood by Luke somehow did not seem

as burdensome as being understood by Robin or Charlie. For one thing, Luke was alone, just like she once thought she wanted to be.

"It doesn't scare you a bit, does it?" she blurted. "To be alone and on your own, I mean."

Luke set High Pockets' hoof down, straightened himself, and put a smile on his face that, when JoBeth thought about it later, seemed more grim than good-natured. "Scare me?" he echoed defiantly. "Naw. It's no big deal. Miss Hattie woulda let me stay down there in Sully City if I'd wanted to. Only I told her it wasn't fair. We weren't blood kin; she didn't owe me. I hope by now she's got herself a new husband. Which would mean she sure don't need me around. So I ain't scared. It's my choice I'm on my own."

But when he glanced past her shoulder a moment later and stared hard at the car parked in front of Mrs. Wilson's office, JoBeth was sure the look in Luke's eyes was one of fear. He touched her arm again, lightly. "You ever seen that car around here before?" he asked softly.

JoBeth turned to stare, too. It was an ordinary-looking car. Tan or gray in color. Not brand-new. There was some writing on the door. "It's probably somebody who's come to talk to Mrs. Wilson about the Benefit," JoBeth decided. "She told me the club would really be busy for the next few weeks."

"Yeah, I s'pose you're right," Luke agreed. There was a smooth, cool note in his voice that surprised JoBeth. She noticed that he didn't take his eyes off the car or Mrs. Wilson's office. "Tell you what, JoBeth, why don't you come back bright and early tomorrow and we'll begin your lessons then? I gotta give High

Pockets a workout yet, then that ol' Sudden Fame who's in the same barn as your sister's horse."

Did she imagine it, or was he anxious to have her gone? "Okay," she agreed, feeling a touch of disappointment. "How early is early? Six A.M. all right?"

"You bet. Then I can get back to my chores by eight, have 'em done before the club gets too busy."

When JoBeth unlocked her bike from the rack in front of Mrs. Wilson's, she made a point of looking at the writing on the door of the car parked there. Kentucky State Board of Corrections. She looked through the window of the office.

Mrs. Wilson appeared to be giving the man inside directions. Whoever he was, he'd no doubt turned off River Road too early. If he was in the corrections business, the place he was looking for was a mile east, up at the Cuyahoga Boys' Correctional Facility.

"Lots of folks figure your first riding lesson begins when you get on your horse," Luke began the next morning. "But it ain't true—or so Perce used to claim. He said first you gotta learn to call things by their right name, beginning with your irons."

Irons? "I guess I don't know what . . ." It made JoBeth feel weird; she was so smart about so many important things—chess and archeology and even cuneiform symbols. Yet here she was, hanging on every soft, southern word uttered by a skinny, none-too-tidy boy with hair blacker than a raven's wing.

"Your stirrups, lady. They're called irons. Didn't they teach you a blamed thing at that Camp Bide-A-Wee place you were telling me about?"

"Bide-A-While," JoBeth corrected. What was I going to learn about irons, she mused, when I spent most of my time reading *Life in a Medieval Castle* cover to cover to Mrs. Culpepper, who probably couldn't have cared less?

"It was my fault I didn't learn more than I did," JoBeth admitted. "I didn't pay any attention to anything they said because I didn't want to. I hated every minute of the whole time I spent in Colorado."

"How come? I mean, I thought you rich types dug that kinda stuff. Summer camps and piano lessons and going fancy places. Perce used to have to teach riding to those kind of kids."

"First off, I'm not a rich kid, as you put it," JoBeth said crisply. "Second of all, I didn't like Colorado because I felt out of place there. Just like I do here at the club, to be honest. Compared to my sister Ashleigh I have two left feet and hands with five thumbs." She'd never admitted that to anyone, not even Robin. She was surprised that saying the words made her feel kind of good.

"Speaking of feet—why don't you stick one of yours into this here iron." Luke held the saddle against his body so that the stirrup rested lightly on the ground at his side. JoBeth had to stand close to him in order to slide her foot into the iron.

"Now if the stirrup is too small, it means you could get hung up in it real easy," Luke explained. "On the other hand, if it's too large, your foot might slip right on through, and if your horse accidentally took a tumble, you could be in a peck of trouble. But look, JoBeth—you got a half an inch on either side of your shoe, see? That's just about right." JoBeth nodded and stepped quickly away from his side. It made her feel sweaty and prickly to stand so close to him. It was pleasing, though, to know that the stirrup probably fit her almost as well as it had Ashleigh.

Then Luke lifted the saddle up and put it across the top rail of the paddock fence. "You know the names of the other parts of your tack?" he asked sternly. "By the way, the word tack means equipment." But JoBeth had to shake her head.

"Well, like I told you, Ol' Perce said a person got smart just about the time he learned to call a thing by its right name. Which was good advice even if he couldn't follow it himself." Luke laid a hand on the top front part of the saddle. "Okay, JoBeth—what's this?"

JoBeth thought hard. She'd only gotten as far as the introduction in her library book. "The front," she answered meekly.

Luke rolled his eyes skyward. "The pommel, that's what it is. And back here, this rise, this is called a cantle." Luke stroked the smooth, flat piece of leather that descended from the top of the saddle. JoBeth saw that Luke's knuckles were scarred and enlarged from hard work. "And this here we call a saddle skirt. The leather straps right here that hold your irons, they're called stirrup leathers. By the way, you use a saddle pad on Rye?"

Rye, who stood beside JoBeth, flicked an ear when he heard his name mentioned. "Golly, I don't know; am I supposed to?"

"Oh, not necessarily. Your saddle is lined and might fit Rye pretty good just the way it is. Some folks call a saddle pad a *numnah*, which is a Fancy Dan word for a flat pad made out of sheepskin or wool felt. If your horse has got a cold back, then you'd probably want to use a pad. That doesn't mean his back is really cold; it means he don't like the slick, cool feel of leather right next to his body. Some horses are fussy, see, just like people can be."

Like I am about scratchy sheets and Teriyaki sauce that leaks into my rice, JoBeth knew. Luke slipped a thumb into the side of Rye's mouth, gently pried it open, and slid the bit in without knocking it against Rye's teeth. "Rest the bit on the bars of your horse's mouth," Luke instructed, and pulled Rye's lip down to show her what he meant.

"The bars—that's what this flat space between his incisors and his molars is called. When you say you've got your horse 'on the bit,' it means you've got the bit positioned right here—and if you've got a real lively horse, sometimes you don't get him on the bit right away and you can't control him—he just takes the bit in his teeth and off he goes." Ah, that explained what had happened in Colorado.

Luke buckled Rye's noseband and made sure it had two fingers worth of space between it and the horse's jawbone. He measured another four fingers of space before cinching up the throat latch. Next, he placed the saddle across Rye's back by setting it high up on the horse's withers and sliding it gently toward the croup.

"Know why I did it that way, JoBeth, instead of just heaving it on any old way?"

"Well . . ." JoBeth thought hard, tried to make sense out of what she'd seen him do. "To make sure Rye's hair lies flat underneath?"

"Atta girl! Otherwise, the horse's hair might get worked up into little clumps, would wear off in patches, and could turn into a saddlesore. Now—get topside and we'll start the next lesson."

Rye stood attentively in the sunshine. JoBeth felt the warmth on the back of her own neck and knew she'd have a fresh crop of freckles by the end of the day. "Take up your reins and grab a fistful of mane if you think you're gonna have a little trouble getting up. With your right hand, take your iron and turn it toward you. Face Rye's rear end, put your left toe into your iron, swing up. . . ."

To her amazement, following his simple directions, JoBeth found herself mounted in one long, smooth, easy effort. She had to smile down at Luke. "You should've seen me that first day," she confessed. "I tried three times before I got up. Nothing I did seemed to work right."

"Bet you faced Rye straight on—which is sorta like climbing a flight of stairs. Now for your dismount: lean forward across Rye's neck and take both feet out of your irons. Brace yourself easy on his neck; swing your right leg over his back. Now let yourself slide to the ground. If your horse bolts now, you won't be hung up, see?"

JoBeth did as she was told but kept her legs stiff and landed hard. "Bend your knees as you come down," Luke suggested. "Now mount up again and let me check your seat."

JoBeth felt her face turn red. Seeing the flush rise out of her collar and into her cheeks made Luke shake his head in mock despair. "Lordy! Living in that museum has softened your brain, lady. I meant your *seat*, JoBeth—or how you sit a horse."

"Oh." JoBeth remounted and felt her cheeks resume their normal color. Luke stepped back four paces. "Think of your seat this way," he advised. "When it's right, a person could look at you sideways like I'm doing now, and could draw a line right down from your earlobe to your hip through to your heel. In other words, JoBeth, you ain't all caved in or swaybacked, either. You're just sitting nice and easy." He squinted at her with professional appraisal.

"And I gotta admit it, JoBeth: You got a pretty good seat." He winked.

JoBeth remembered Charlie's wink. She'd had the feeling Charlie expected her to giggle and get coy. But Luke was different. Rather like she was herself. Didn't quite fit into life the way he was supposed to. JoBeth winked back.

"By the way," she said, a grin turning up the corners of her mouth, "you were wondering about that tan car yesterday? It must've belonged to somebody who'd taken the wrong turnoff. It was a man from Kentucky who was looking for that boys' reformatory up the road." A moment ago, Luke's words had made her blush. Now, JoBeth was surprised to see that hers made Luke seem to pale under his tan and nibble thoughtfully at his lower lip.

9

Luke's commands, always given in his soft, southern drawl, haunted JoBeth's sleep at night and followed her through the Archer every afternoon.

"Keep your head up!"

"Don't look at them hands, JoBeth! Would you drive a car by staring at the steering wheel?"

"Back straight, lady; heels down!"

Drill, drill, drill—but at the end of three days she got permission to trot, and JoBeth felt like she'd gratuated from kindergarten into first grade.

Learning to post was a chore, however. She was sure she'd never get the hang of it. "Rise on the diagonal from your *knees*," Luke kept saying. "Don't haul yourself up with your reins like that! By the way, JoBeth, you wanta know where the word 'post' comes from? In the olden days, postmen had to make the mail rounds in good time. But to ride all day at a trot is hard—until some bright guy learned to rise out of his saddle on the first beat, drop back on the second, then do it all over again. Pretty soon that technique just got to be called 'posting.' "

No sooner did JoBeth think she was posting pretty well than Luke informed her she did it too well. "I see way too much daylight between you and that cantle, JoBeth. The idea of posting is just to keep you from beating your kidneys to death, or your horse's—not to hang yourself on some sky hook!"

Finally, exasperated, Luke called out: "Hop down a minute, JoBeth, and let me show you how to do it." Then he was up on Rye himself, and put the yellow horse into a smart trot with only the slightest impulsion from his legs. He rose to post with a motion that barely lifted his buttocks off the cantle; he seemed to be more a part of Rye than an ornament on top of him. Horse and rider went briskly down the fence, turned, came up the far side.

Luke loves what he's doing, JoBeth realized with a pang. He *lives* riding. . . . But what I do at the museum, maybe I do so I'll get rewarded. Patted on the head. Told what a good little girl I am. . . .

When Luke halted Rye a moment later at her side, he was grinning broadly. "Say—he's just the dandiest little horse! I told you that you were lucky, didn't I? And you know what we oughta do now? I'll go get High Pockets and we'll ride together. If you can get your post down a little better, I'll even show you how to canter."

JoBeth wondered if she was ready for anything more. Her thighs ached from trying to post properly. The back of her neck was wet with sweat. Her knees were sore; her ankles were stiff. But when she joined Luke on one of the bridle paths, she found energy enough to listen to him explain how to achieve a canter.

"Rye'll need you to tell him what you want from

him, JoBeth. You can't expect him to read your mind. So after you get into a trot, tell him you want more speed by pressing both calves firmly into his sides. Don't kick him—that's how they do it in the movies. A good rider is easier on his horse. As soon as Rye gets your message, he'll change stride from a one-two gait to a one-three gait. Then all you have to do is sit back and relax, because a canter is like rocking in your grandmother's rocking chair."

JoBeth couldn't remember her grandmother's rocker, but that's just what a canter felt like: it was an easy, soothing gait very much different from a trot. JoBeth felt the wind in her face. The museum, the stone pony, being her father's daughter, Queen Victoria's linen chest—none of them mattered as hugely as they had a week ago. What mattered most was being out in the sunshine with a boy in a blue shirt, learning how to ride Ashleigh's horse.

Two weeks later, after Rye and High Pockets had been rubbed down and their stalls had been mucked out and spread with fresh oat straw, JoBeth realized yet another day had come to a close. Her parents would be along soon to take her home; they'd put her bike on the car rack as they used to do for Ashleigh. Then they'd all stop for a treat at the Dairy Queen.

"You need a ride home, Luke?" Maybe he'd like something from the Dairy Queen, too.

"Home?" He glanced away when she said the word. "Naw. That's okay. It ain't much of a walk. If I want to go anyplace else, I just go on my thumb. You know— hitch." He gave her a look that surprised her: Once again, it was wary and suspicious. "How come you're so interested all of a sudden about where I live?"

JoBeth blinked. "I wasn't trying to be nosy," she snapped, hurt. "I thought I'd do you a favor, that's all. Save you a long walk. Or whatever. Forget I mentioned it."

In the soft evening light, Luke's gray eyes were ringed with green at their outer edges, giving his whole face a wild, unpredictable look. JoBeth turned on her heel and walked away. Maybe they'd been together so much lately they were getting on each other's nerves.

"Listen, I'm sorry," came Luke's voice from behind her back. She waited in mid-stride for him to go on. "If you wanta know where I live, I'll show you."

"My folks'll be here any minute," JoBeth muttered. "I don't have time to . . ."

"Oh, it won't take long. On account of I live right here."

JoBeth turned around. She looked past him to the club grounds—to the building where Mrs. Wilson had her office, to the horse barns, the bridle paths, the obstacle courses with their whitewashed fences. "But there isn't any *here* here," she protested.

"Sure, there is. You just can't see it, that's all. You don't know what to look for, that's why. C'mon, I'll show you."

One by one, all the uncertainties she'd always had about Luke began to surface in JoBeth's mind: he looked hunted; he was a school dropout; he didn't know the difference between cirrhosis and sirocco.

But when Luke motioned her to follow, JoBeth let herself fall into step beside him. They left Rye's barn, walked along the fence that enclosed the main exercise ring. They went past the next barn and the next one, to the last barn along the concourse. JoBeth could see that it was much older than any of the others, needed a coat of paint, and was missing a few shingles on its roof.

"Practically nobody uses this barn anymore," Luke told her, "maybe only for extra tack when they have a show."

JoBeth glanced over her shoulder toward Rye's barn. It seemed uncomfortably far away. The club office, too, was tiny and white in the evening distance. In front of her, Luke's shoulders were sharp and thin under his soiled shirt. Out here, even the shadows in the grass seemed darker. JoBeth started to breathe fast and told herself to slow down, to take it easy.

"What's wrong?" Luke asked. "You scared or something?"

"No," JoBeth lied, "I was just checking to see if my folks'd got here yet. I better not take too long, though; they don't like to have to wait for me."

Luke entered the barn and led her down the dim aisle. He halted unexpectedly in front of the next-to-last stall at the end. "Well, here it is," he announced. "Home Sweet Home."

Except for being older, the box stall they stood in front of wasn't much different from the newer ones Rye and High Pockets occupied. The bottom half was made of tongue-and-groove pine boards; the top half was wire mesh. The inside of the stall was dark, and it was impossible to see what it held. A coolness chilled the back of JoBeth's neck. Luke stepped in front of her and slid the door of the stall open.

"Look inside," he invited. "It ain't so bad. You better believe this man's boy has lately lived in a whole lot worse."

JoBeth peeked into the stall. In one dim corner was

a saggy camp cot with no pillow and only a single olive-green blanket to cover it. A round, twenty-five pound fiberboard container that once held molasses pellets had been turned upside down to make a table. Two paperback detective novels rested on a two-by-four wall brace. Next to them was a bottle of black hair dye. A shirt, nearly as soiled as the one Luke was wearing, hung on a nail beside the open door.

"This is where you live?" JoBeth whispered. The bunkhouse at the Bide-A-While had been a palace by comparison.

"Yep." There was a pleased sense of ownership in Luke's voice that, on second thought, made perfectly good sense to JoBeth. Maybe he felt about the horse stall the way she felt about living alone at the Archer.

"When winter comes, though, I reckon I'll have to chuck it and find a warmer place. Even now, some mornings when it's real damp, I get up feeling as stiff and sore as Ol' Perce used to."

"I bet Mrs. Wilson doesn't know you live back here."

" 'Course she doesn't. You promise not to tell her?"

"Why'd you show all this to me in the first place if you thought I'd tell Mrs. Wilson in the second place?"

Luke studied her silently. "You wanta know why? Remember that first day I saw you, when I was taking High Pockets over caviletti?" So that's what those white-painted poles laid out on the ground were called. JoBeth nodded, but didn't take her eyes from Luke's face.

"I got the feeling that day, it's sorta hard to put into words, that you were like me, JoBeth." He peered hopefully into her eyes. His own were no longer green-ringed and wild. "See, the look on your face that day was like I feel inside sometimes. *You* know: lost, kind of." He had been looking for someone, too.

Luke leaned back against the door and scraped some tanbark in the aisle of the barn into a pyramid with the toe of his dirty yellow boot. "Oh, I know you ain't really lost or anything like that," he admitted. "You got a family; even had a sister once. So maybe I was kidding myself. After all, you're a person who knows an artifact is a product of primitive human workmanship," he finished with a rueful smile.

JoBeth smiled too, and didn't care if her lips kept her braces covered or not. She was sure he hadn't even listened to her that night! To realize he had made her feel impulsive.

"I can wash clothes, too," she said, "and tomorrow I'll bring this back all fresh and clean." With that, JoBeth picked his soiled shirt off its nail in the wall. She gasped and took two astonished steps backward when Luke snatched it back out of her hands an instant later. Once again, fear made two hard, green emeralds out of Luke's eyes.

But he was too late. JoBeth saw the label sewn into the collar of the shirt. It was made out of that same white twill tape Mother used to mark her and Ashleigh's clothes when they went to Colorado. Except the label in Luke's shirt didn't bear his name. Instead, the black stenciled letters clearly read: *Property of the Kentucky Boys' Home.*

"You saw . . . didn't you?"

Luke's question was so sad and soft she could hardly hear his words. Regret had bleached all the green out of his gray eyes. He clamped his mouth shut so tight

JoBeth saw two white marks enclose his lips like parentheses.

She wondered if she should shake her head and deny having seen a thing. He might even believe her. After all, wearing a mask was still her special talent.

"Yes, I did," she admitted instead. To blurt the words right out like that made her face feel naked. Having taken that much of a risk, JoBeth decided to confess something else. "I think I already knew there was something different about you, Luke. When I saw that the tan car belonged to someone from the Board of Corrections in Kentucky, I tried to convince both of us he'd taken the wrong turnoff, that he really meant to stop up the road at the CBF. But he *was* looking for you, wasn't he, Luke?"

Luke nodded.

"Did you run away from some place? A reformatory, or a place like the CBF?"

"Sort of."

"Sort of? Either you did or you didn't, Luke."

Luke tipped his head back and stared into the darkness of the rafters overhead. "Yeah, I ran away all right," he groaned. "It wasn't hard to do. It was a minimum-security kind of place. No high walls or barbed wire or anything like that. Actually, it was like a farm. We raised corn, beans, and tomatoes. They didn't have any horses, though. So I just walked away one day. And kept right on walking." He gave her a wan smile.

"Which explains why you're here," JoBeth prodded the way Dr. Morris had prodded at her, "but it doesn't explain why you got put there to begin with."

"It was simple, lady. I didn't have a job. Or folks. I didn't tell anybody about Miss Hattie; anyway, she ain't real kin. I was practically what the judge called an orphan. Under eighteen, too. And I got caught stealing."

It was JoBeth's turn to smile wanly. "I suppose that'd do it, all right."

"Food, that's what I stole," Luke confessed. "A loaf of raisin bread and some cheese. In Louisville, that's where. I didn't get a bite before that store manager had me by the collar." JoBeth peered over Luke's shoulder to the grounds beyond the door. The courtryside was shrouded in darkness, and she was sure she saw a pair of car lights turn into the long drive that led to Mrs. Wilson's office.

"After Perce died, JoBeth, I just didn't know what to do," Luke explained. "He wasn't much, I guess, him and his cough medicine, but he was all I had. So I took to drifting. Figured I'd make my own way, y'know. Worked a time at some stables near Louisville. Later at Lexington. Always had to move on, though, soon as somebody started snooping around."

"Ever thought about going back, Luke? Doing your time, or whatever it's called?"

Luke avoided her glance. "The cheese was that kind where every slice is wrapped up nice in its own piece of cellophane," he said dreamily, ignoring her question.

He's as mixed up as I am, JoBeth thought, and can't even give me a straight answer. "Well, if it'll make you feel any better," she offered, "I've thought about doing the same thing myself."

Luke seemed amazed. "Why'd a person like you ever want to steal bread and cheese?" he marveled.

"Oh, I don't mean about stealing food. I mean

about going off to live by myself. Once I decided to live the rest of my life in a closet at the Archer."

She made it sound like a decision she'd made years ago, instead of only weeks ago. "I figured I'd hide where we keep the Early American quilts stored when they aren't on display. I even picked out a bed—in Queen Victoria's linen chest. I got in it one night to see how it fit."

"Weird," Luke breathed. "What'd it feel like?"

"Raisin-bread-and-cheese thieves are not entitled to talk about weird," JoBeth advised him. Then she decided to tell him what it *had* felt like: "It felt just like a coffin, Luke. Because that's what I wanted to be. Dead."

She'd never been tempted to admit anything like that to Dr. Morris. Or Father. Or anyone. But Luke seemed just as puzzled as JoBeth had been afraid others would be. "You are a person who's practically rich, whether she wants to admit it or not," he objected. "A person who's got her own horse, even if it did belong to her sister first. Got folks, a job, things that count. So why would that kind of a person ever want to be *dead*?"

"Because it wasn't fair that Ashleigh had to be the one," JoBeth said. "My sister was the one who had everything, Luke, not me. Everyone liked her. Dogs, cats, and horses, of course. And have you ever noticed how it is with golden people? They just keep getting golder all the time. Pretty soon, people like that are enough to blind your eyes."

All the while she talked, JoBeth kept her eyes fastened on Luke's. If he looked horrified or full of pity, she'd stop in mid-sentence. But he studied her quietly and waited for her to go on.

"The worst thing, though, is that I can't actually remember anymore what Ashleigh really looked like. Sometimes I can see her hair—it was very long and was different shades of yellow—but I can't see her face anymore. She's sort of invisible. One night, I climbed into her bed. I thought it'd help me remember. Only I went to sleep instead. Finding me there the next morning practically made a basket case out of my mother. She decided I'd have to see a shrink."

"You mean one of them guys who tries to rearrange a person's brains?"

JoBeth nodded.

"Here, lemme see," Luke said, and laid a mocking hand across the top of her head. His fingers, spread fanwise, covered her whole crown. "Too bad," he lamented, "them brains still feel pretty loose to Dr. Luke."

He smiled ruefully and, as if it were the most natural thing to do, laced the fingers of both hands together to make a hoop out of his arms. He let it drop gently over JoBeth's shoulders. She stiffened. From her window upstairs, she'd seen Ashleigh hug Dizzy Johnson on the front step; sometimes Ashleigh had even cupped his face in her hands and kissed him goodnight. JoBeth had always known for sure she could never do anything like that herself.

She was surprised to discover how easy it was to link her own hands together behind Luke's back and lay her cheek over his heart. She felt its steady beat an inch under her ear. Was this how people felt when they stopped being a nobody-knows-me person, kind of warm and happy? Along with everything else, maybe Luke was a mindreader, too, for JoBeth heard him murmur over the top of her head: "See, JoBeth, I was right. You and me, we *are* alike. Except neither one of us is lost anymore. Now we got each other."

A car horn sounded in the drive beside Mrs. Wilson's office. JoBeth jumped out of the circle of Luke's arms. She snatched his shirt off the ground where he'd dropped it. "You gonna come back tomorrow?" Luke whispered. But JoBeth was already running toward the car lights, rolling his shirt into a ball as she went. *Oh, yes, Luke, I'll be back,* she wanted to call to him but couldn't because each step carried her closer to her parents' car. *We got each other now, and I'll be back for sure.*

Before she climbed into bed, JoBeth showered and gave her hair a hundred strokes. Her hair was so short it didn't take very long. She leaned toward the image in the mirror. Her eyes, almond-shaped and tipped up at their outer corners, seemed almost pretty.

Robin wore contacts now, had gotten some six months ago. JoBeth remembered how disgusted she'd felt. Rob is like every other girl at Everly High. Wants to look good for some guy, she'd thought. It seemed like such a dimwitted wish. JoBeth smiled sheepishly at the girl in the mirror. Well, she might have to reconsider. Maybe she'd get contacts herself someday. Not real soon, of course; but someday.

JoBeth squinted nearsightedly and leaned closer to the mirror. There was something above her left eyebrow. She tugged at it. It was a silver hair.

JoBeth frowned and stepped back. The image in the mirror got fuzzy. Well. She'd wait so long for that first silver strand. It was part of that old kindred spirit business. But how come it wasn't more exciting?

JoBeth tumbled her hair briskly with her fingers so the silver hair was buried by brown ones.

"I'll have to get some of that Grecian Formula stuff to cover it up awhile," she told the girl in the mirror who somehow did not look quite like the girl she used to know. JoBeth remembered the bottle of black hair dye next to the two detective novels in Luke's hideaway. She wondered what color *his* hair really was.

10

"Is it okay with you if I haul some stuff to eat out to the club?" JoBeth asked. Before her mother had a chance to think about it, JoBeth was on her knees in front of the bottom cupboard fishing for food she especially liked: Vienna sausages ... olives stuffed with pimiento ... corn curls ... Oreos ... pop-top cans of butterscotch pudding.

"Of course you can, JoBeth, but if I fixed a better breakfast maybe you wouldn't have to . . ."

"Oh, it isn't that, Mother. It's just that sometimes I get hungry when I'm out there. Learning how to ride is harder work than I ever figured it would be. I decided it might give me some extra pep to have something around to snack on."

"Is there a place at the club where all of it will be safe, JoBeth?"

"Sure. I'll just stick everything in my—I mean, Ashleigh's—locker." Everything was destined to end up in a place Luke called Home Sweet Home, but JoBeth decided not to get into that. In her room, she packed the provisions in her backpack. She cushioned the cans on top of some old towels she'd taken from a shelf in the bathroom closet. She slipped a bar of soap into one of the side pockets of the pack along with samples of shampoo and toothpaste that'd come in the mail but nobody in the house had bothered to use.

Last to be packed was Luke's clean shirt. JoBeth had cut the label out of the shirt as soon as she got home the night before, and flushed it down the toilet. She washed the shirt by hand in the bathroom she once shared with Ashleigh, then hung it up to dry in the shower stall with the curtain pulled shut.

Getting the pack organized took longer than she'd planned, and Mother had already gone to play tennis with Mrs. Dalrymple before JoBeth wheeled out of the driveway. When she pedaled past the Greenwillow Recreation Club, JoBeth could see the two women playing on the court nearest the street. Mother played with more determination than Mrs. Dalrymple. Or maybe she's still solving problems by wearing herself to a frazzle, JoBeth mused.

JoBeth slowed her bike at the curb to watch as her mother rose on tiptoe and smacked a fast serve low over the net. Poor, plump Mrs. D. missed it by a mile. JoBeth whistled. Her mother turned, trim and tan; she waved her racquet victoriously in the air.

JoBeth noticed the plum-colored blush of a varicose vein on her mother's tan thigh. She doesn't really look as much like Ashleigh as I always used to think, JoBeth decided. In fact, Carol Cunningham could pass for anybody's tall, tan, forty-five-year-old tennis-mad mother. *Any*body's mother? JoBeth corrected herself wryly. *Your* mother, you dope.

JoBeth shoved off from the curb with her toe. When

are you going to learn to look at people as they really are? she asked herself as she pedaled toward the club. You've worn a mask so long, J.B., that you feel happier when everyone else wears one, too. It's like you're so scared about knowing yourself you don't want to know anybody else either. Awesome possibilities. She made up her mind not to make such mistakes with Luke.

JoBeth reached back to check her hip pocket. The notebook was still there. Not that merely hauling it back and forth to the club each day did her much good. Doubts about ever being able to decode the script on the stone pony began to nag at JoBeth, and the day seemed less sunny. Every night for two weeks she'd rescued the horse from his meadow in the diorama, but the marks on his stomach still defied any effort she made to decipher them.

"I just know it has something to do with the constellation Orion," she muttered, "because if it doesn't, my hunch is . . ." *All wrong,* her scientific self warned her. JoBeth slowed her bike; she didn't want to think about Schliemann's opinion of people who tried to make history fit hunches.

JoBeth's lips were chapped; she moistened them lightly with her tongue. It was hard to push the suspicion out of her mind: Maybe what I thought was a hunch wasn't that at all. Maybe it was only a *wish.* A wish to be kindred spirits with my father, to have him forget what happened to Ashleigh. I guess I wanted him to smile again, see little fans at the corners of his eyes, have him tell me how clever I was. It seemed to be a morning for awesome thoughts to gang up on a person.

The straps of the pack dug into JoBeth's shoulders. In the green distance she could see the white fences and immaculate trails of the club. But things were different now. A few weeks ago, it was enough to caress the stone horse and weave cool safe dreams around him. But now a sturdy yellow horse with a hide like warm satin waited for her, not to mention a boy whose last name she didn't even know and whose hair color was still a secret. JoBeth smiled and began to pedal a little faster.

"Watch the point of Rye's shoulder, JoBeth!" Luke called. "His leading foreleg will move out ahead of the opposite shoulder." JoBeth leaned over to get a better look. "No, no, not like that!" Luke bellowed. "First thing you know you're gonna take a header right off him!" JoBeth straightened up, redfaced.

"Well, it's hard to tell which lead he's on," she complained. "How else am I supposed to know if I don't lean over to see?"

"It'll get easier after awhile," Luke promised her. "What you gotta do, JoBeth, is concentrate on feeling, not looking. If you do glance down, though, it can't be any more than a flick of your eyeballs, because any judge in the country will mark you down for dropping your chin even a smidge. Remember the old saying, heads up and heels down. You won't go wrong if you do."

Luke rode beside her on High Pockets and monitored her every move. She wondered why he didn't mind all the time he spent with her until one day he told her why it suited him: "Teaching you does two things, JoBeth. Gives *you* a good start—and helps *me* with High Pockets. He gets nice and loose while I'm drilling you, and after you're gone, he's ready to jump like he means business. Otherwise, he's uptight and acts more like a stargazer than ever."

"C'mon, Luke. Not even High Pockets can see stars in the middle of the morning."

"That just means he keeps his nose up all the time. Fact is, I asked Mrs. Wilson to check with Mr. Blasing and see if I can put a martingale on High Pockets to bring that nose out of the sky. It's a habit that could get him—or Mr. Blasing—in a lot of trouble. You can't take a fence good, you know, unless you're looking at it instead of at the sky."

"I've never seen you jump High Pockets. You watch me ride all the time, but it's never been the other way around."

"You want to watch me jump him?" The idea seemed to please Luke. When JoBeth nodded that she would, Luke said, "Well, first off, let me shorten my stirrup leathers a hole or two." He took his foot out of his iron, moved his leg easily up along High Pockets' shoulder, quickly readjusted the leather on his near side, then did the same on the right side.

"Knees and ankles are even more important in jumping than they are in park riding," he explained. "They act sort of like shock absorbers do on a car. With your stirrup leathers shortened, you get more spring action in your joints."

JoBeth rode beside him to the end of the practice ring where a three-foot jump had been set up. Luke motioned JoBeth toward the infield while he moved at a purposeful, collected trot downfield. But he didn't take the jump immediately; instead, he turned High Pockets back, moved the big bay out of a collected trot into a collected canter, and approached the jump again.

When High Pockets was about as far from the jump as it was high, or about three feet, JoBeth saw Luke glide his hand along the horse's neck, giving him more freedom on the rein while at the same time keeping him on the bit.

The bay raised his head slightly, gathered his back legs underneath himself, and rose in the air. He traced a long, smooth trajectory over the hurdle with neck extended downward and all four legs tucked neatly beneath himself. Just before the point of landing, High Pockets shortened his neck, raised his head, and struck out with both forelegs. He came down first on his near leg; the off leg followed a second later. Luke, who'd been in precise control the whole time, seemed hardly to have moved at all.

"Is that as easy as you make it look?" JoBeth marveled after horse and rider cantered back to the infield.

Luke gave her a smug grin. "A pro can make anything look easy," he boasted.

"Doesn't it bother you that you'll never get to show High Pockets yourself? It'll be Mr. Blasing who gets all the glory. Mrs. Wilson and I are about the only ones who'll ever know High Pockets is good because *you* made him good."

Luke shrugged. "Why should it bother me? I get paid to do something I really like to do." But he paused, as if her question had stirred up some old doubts. "Well, sure, I reckon it'd be dandy if I could show the old stargazer myself. Except I'd only be what the rule book calls an agent, since I don't own High Pockets myself. Which means if we won a ribbon together, it'd belong to Mr. Blasing anyhow."

"But it doesn't seem fair," JoBeth insisted. She watched Luke pull his fingers through his inky hair.

113

In the sunlight his eyes were clear and seemed to keep no secrets.

"A lot of things in this life ain't fair, JoBeth," he reminded her gently. "You oughta know that better'n anybody I can think of."

Each morning JoBeth practiced her posting for at least thirty minutes. She soon learned that Rye's trot, whether it was a slow one or a fast one, was executed at a precise one-two, one-two rhythm. "You're lucky you got a horse with a square trot," Luke told her the first week they worked together, "because it's a lot easier to post to than a trot that's either too long or too short."

A square trot, he explained later, meant that Rye's diagonal legs—for example, his right front leg and left hind leg—struck the ground at exactly the same moment, one hoof neither ahead nor behind its mate. JoBeth finally got the knack of flicking a glance at Rye's shoulder without actually bending her head, too; when the point of his shoulder moved back, she settled into the saddle with a rolling motion of her thighs, then rose to post when the shoulder moved forward.

When Rye went into a fast trot, she learned to come forward by leaning a bit from the hips in order to keep her balance perfect. It was easier to do, she noticed, if she was careful to keep her heels directly under her own center of gravity. If she was able to do that, it meant she could settle against the cantle at the exact moment to meet the forward thrust of Rye's leg movement, both of which pushed her automatically back into a posting position without requiring that she mechanically push her weight out of the saddle.

Luke had told her that the first thing she'd have to do in the ring in front of a judge was mount and dismount, so JoBeth started each day with ten minutes' practice of those two routines. Each time, she felt a quiet astonishment: the muscles in the calf of her right leg bunched to prepare for the upward thrust; and when she dismounted, she felt the muscles of her abdomen tighten as she leaned across Rye's neck and swung her leg over the point of his croup.

"Those're muscles I didn't even know I owned until I came out here," she had to admit. "The only one I ever used before was the one between my ears."

One morning as she put Rye through his paces around the practice ring, JoBeth noticed something else: there were two scabs on the knuckle of her right thumb, and all ten fingernails were split and grimy.

Not exactly your average scholar's hands, she mused. Last week, Mother had even suggested her neck might be dirty, but when JoBeth pulled down the collar of her shirt, the supposed dirt turned out to be a ring of suntan.

"Suntan!" Carol Cunningham had exclaimed in disbelief. Gee, does she think she's the only person who can have one? JoBeth wondered.

"Maybe it isn't really a tan," she'd heard herself answer peevishly. "Maybe my freckles just moved closer together."

Her mother had squeezed her shoulder. "Tan or freckles, it doesn't matter, darling. Lately, you've just been . . . oh, I don't know, kind of like your old self. But different, too. You never used to make jokes, you know—let alone get brown."

JoBeth shrugged, embarrassed by her mother's attention. "I guess I didn't make jokes before because

115

I'm sort of a serious person. I suppose you could actually say I've always been sort of deadly serious."

Her mother's smile dimmed a bit at the use of that word, deadly. JoBeth wished she could explain it wasn't as bad as it sounded. There were lots of things that used to be true that weren't anymore, not since she'd met Luke. Luke, of course, was something else hard to explain. For instance, wouldn't it prompt another anxious call to Dr. Morris if she were to suddenly announce, "The person who's teaching me how to ride this summer is an escaped bread-and-cheese thief"?

It was like she told Luke: There wasn't any "sort of" about being a thief. Either you were or you weren't. He was. JoBeth had a vague feeling she ought to be less forgiving of what Luke had done. Stealing *was* stealing, after all. But what matters most is that he's started to fill up the holes in my life, she told herself, the ones Ashleigh left behind.

At ten thirty JoBeth finished working Rye and walked him slowly back to the barn to cool him off. The inside of the barn was dim after the brightness of the outdoors. She stripped the saddle from Rye's back and put a sweat sheet on him. After she'd mucked out his stall and drawn a bucket of fresh water, she placed the palm of her hand in the crescent-shaped, muscled area between his front legs as Luke had shown her how to do. The horse was neither too warm nor too cool, and she put him back in his stall.

JoBeth glanced around for Luke and was glad she couldn't see him. He was probably still out with High Pockets, which meant she had plenty of time to run over to Home Sweet Home and get things ready for the celebration.

He'd been crazy about the food and towels and toothpaste she brought before; he'd be even more astonished now by the party she'd planned. It was four weeks since he'd walked into the Archer on that rainy night with an offer about riding lessons; it was time to let him know how grateful she felt. They'd celebrate together with Twinkies and two cans of Mountain Dew (Ralph Smith's aunt gave her another sad look), plus some yellow plates and cups to dress up Luke's fiberboard table.

Everything was ready when JoBeth heard Luke's footsteps in the tanbark aisle outside Home Sweet Home. When he pushed the stall door aside, his gray eyes got wide. "Lordy, what's all this? Whose birthday is it? Mine ain't until January twelfth. . . ."

JoBeth felt her cheeks get warm. "People can celebrate things besides birthdays," she said. "This is an anniversary. I didn't want to pass it off just like any old day of the week, Luke. Today, see, we've been friends for four whole weeks."

Luke grinned crookedly. "Then we got *two* things to celebrate, JoBeth! On account of Mrs. Wilson just now asked me if I'd be willing to ride High Pockets in the Benefit. Mr. Blasing's been on vacation and came home with something called hepatitis. He's in the hospital and won't be out until the show's long over."

JoBeth sat on the edge of Luke's cot and fidgeted with the hem of the drab green blanket that covered it. She realized a glad smile should've leaped instantly to her face. But it didn't, a fact Luke noticed, too.

"Hey—I thought you'd be even happier'n me, JoBeth. Ain't you the one who said it'd be neat if I

117

could show High Pockets instead of Mr. Blasing? But now you look like the news was worse'n ten miles of bad road. How come?"

"Well, it *seems* like good news," JoBeth agreed slowly, trying to decide just how to phrase her objections. "But the way Mrs. Wilson talks, a lot of people will turn out for the Benefit. Which means that guy in the tan car might show up again, too. Especially since he knows you like to hang out any place there are horses. Which also means, Luke, if you ride High Pockets into the show ring you might end up right back in Kentucky in that reformatory."

Luke tapped his thigh lightly with his fist. "I already thought about all that, JoBeth." He chewed on his lower lip, then sat down on the edge of the cot beside her.

"Here's the deal, JoBeth: High Pockets is already a grade one, which means he's got more'n seventy competition points. He's far and away the best horse this boy's ever had a chance to ride. And with that martingale Mr. Blasing let me put on him, the old fool is jumping well enough to clear the moon!" "Old fool" was said with affection, and JoBeth saw Luke's eyes glow with pleasure.

"But you don't even have the right kind of clothes for going into the show ring," JoBeth pointed out. "They're expensive, those kinds of outfits; Ashleigh needed that stuff, so I know how much it costs. That's all she and Mother talked about for a month. You have to have a fitted coat and a hat and good boots." JoBeth leaned over and glanced with raised eyebrows at Luke's runover yellow ones.

Luke turned a quizzical gray gaze on her. "Hey. I can't believe it. Ain't *you* the one who mentioned me going back to do my time in Kentucky? Now all of a sudden you're singing a different tune. Worried I might get caught and all that. What changed your mind?"

A pinched feeling crossed JoBeth's forehead. The muscles along her jaw got tight. She'd almost forgotten what it felt like to wear a mask. When you love, you take the risk you might lose what you love, Dr. Morris warned her. If Luke went away now, she'd be full of holes again. "I just think if you stay out of sight like you've been doing, Luke, you might go unnoticed until they quit looking for you. You could stay right here forever."

Luke reached over and laid two fingers against her cheek. He forced her to look him in the eye. "Nothing lasts forever, JoBeth," he reminded her softly. She lowered her lashes and refused to look at him. "JoBeth, you gotta understand: I ain't like your little stone pony," he went on. "I decided even before Mrs. Wilson talked to me this morning that I couldn't live my life in a glass cage where the rocks are made out of styrofoam and the only mountains a person ever sees are ones painted on a plaster wall."

"You've got no right to say that!" JoBeth cried indignantly and jumped to her feet. She knew her cheeks were red. "I got you toothpaste and Twinkies and now all you want to do is . . ." She stopped short. *Betrayed.* Why did that word pop right into her head again?

"I do so have a right, JoBeth," Luke insisted. He got up and reached for her hand. His callused fingers were warm, but she snatched her own away. "We're friends, JoBeth. *You* even wanted to celebrate the fact!

119

Being friends means I got a right to be honest with you."

He caught her hand again and wouldn't let it go. "Perce and my own daddy couldn't be honest with me, JoBeth. They kept right on calling that stuff cough medicine which everybody knew it sure wasn't. But I don't want to do that to you, JoBeth."

"Well, I think *I* made another mistake," JoBeth snapped and was amazed at the bitterness in her voice. "I should've been spending my time trying to decode that writing on the stone pony instead of trying to learn how to ride some dumb horse. Once I thought you looked like a picture of someone in a book at the museum and now you don't want to . . ."

"JoBeth, I'm not someone in a book. I'm *me*! A guy who made things worse for himself by trying to make 'em better. Sooner or later, both you and me know I'm gonna have to finish my time at the boys' home. But first I'm gonna ride me a winner, JoBeth!"

"They'll catch you. They'll take you away. It'll be just like it was with Ashleigh."

JoBeth heard Luke make a crooning sound like the one Mother made the night in the music room when Father cried. He made another hoop out of his arms and let it drop over her shoulders.

"Nobody's talking about dying, JoBeth," he said, and pulled her close. "All I want to do is ride a stargazer over a few jumps, help him get some more points." Luke hugged her, but JoBeth didn't link her arms around his waist.

"Quit being so doggone serious about everything that comes along," Luke urged. "In fact, you oughta start tonight: somebody's set up a carnival down the road apiece, between the club and that Cuyahoga whatever-its-name is. They got everything a carnival oughta have—pitchball and a Ferris wheel and fortune tellers. So let's you and me go over there tonight. We'll eat hot dogs and cotton candy and act like two ordinary folks without a care in the world. C'mon, JoBeth, say yes."

JoBeth shut her eyes, linked her arms suddenly around Luke, and hung onto him hard. She'd take the risk. But he was wrong about one thing: They weren't ordinary at all. He was a runaway from a reformatory. And she was still trying to find out who JoBeth Cunningham really was.

By the time JoBeth got downstairs after supper, she discovered Mother had already left to attend a meeting of the Women's Tennis Association. Father was surprised that she, too, intended to go out. "At this hour, JoBeth?" He glanced at his watch. "It's nearly eight o'clock—but judging from those jeans I'd say you were thinking about going back to the club."

"There's a carnival set up nearby," JoBeth explained. "I was going to stop there after I check Rye's hoof. He seemed a little lame today," she fibbed.

"Well, I don't think it's a good idea for you to be riding your bike that far at this hour, or worse, riding it home later." He laid his book aside and tamped his pipe with fresh tobacco. "But it's no trouble for me to drive you out. Maybe I'll even go to the carnival with you."

A few weeks ago it would've been the best news he could've given her. "Gosh, I was going to meet a friend and we were going to . . ."

Dr. Cunningham shrugged agreeably. "No problem, JoBeth." He picked up his book. "I'll just take this along and read it while you're at the carnival. We can pick up your friend on the way, if you'd like. Robin, is it?"

"No, it's someone . . . someone I met at the club this summer."

"Fine! Your mother and I have been so glad to see you busy, JoBeth!"

Your mother and I. It was once an expression he rarely used. Instead, it used to be: "Want to run down to the museum with me, JoBeth? Mother and Ashleigh are off to play tennis." Or badminton or golf or whatever. But those were the balanced times, JoBeth thought as her father backed the car out of the drive. She peeked at his profile; he had an aquiline nose and a pronounced crest at the brow line. Luke didn't have a profile like a Highland prince, of course. His nose was short and snubbed on the end, and his brow line was smooth.

Dr. Cunningham turned, aware that he was being studied. "You're awfully quiet tonight, JoBeth. You used to chatter up a storm on rides like this. The museum, some article you read in the *National Geographic*—my word, you always had so much to talk about!"

"I guess I haven't been doing much reading this summer," JoBeth apologized. "I'm too tired after riding Rye all morning and working all afternoon at the Archer."

"Speaking of the Archer—how are you coming with that project Miss Malowan told me about?"

"What project?" So they'd been talking about her again.

"Oh, Mag seems to think you might be trying to decode the script on that artifact we got from Luristan

122

last year. You know, the stone pony. But maybe she was mistaken."

"Oh, she was right, all right," JoBeth mumbled. She wondered if she should tell him her hunch had turned out to be wrong, that the marks on the stomach of the stone horse apparently had nothing to do with the constellation of Orion after all.

"I remember how you and Ashleigh liked to hear that story about Orion's belt," he mused as if he could read her mind. JoBeth stiffened and fussed needlessly with her seat belt. The news that Ashleigh had liked that story too was an unwelcome surprise.

"I didn't know Ashleigh was much interested in that kind of stuff," JoBeth said, and stared straight ahead.

"Oh, I don't think she ever had quite the same deep interest in the museum that you always have, JoBeth. But when she was quite little—before you were born and then when you were still a baby—Ashleigh used to come to the museum with me on Saturday mornings. It was only after you started school and got so interested in the museum yourself that she began to play tennis and spend so much time with Mother."

After he parked near the carnival grounds, JoBeth leaned over to give her father a hasty peck on the cheek. He patted her hand. "You and your girlfriend have a good time, JoBeth. See you in an hour or so." *Your girlfriend.* He assumed she couldn't have any other kind. But that was not as upsetting as his implication that Ashleigh was not as different from herself as she'd always thought. JoBeth pushed that possibility out of her mind and hurried toward the carnival lights. She hoped Luke would not be hard to spot in the crowd.

The Luke she finally spied was one she hardly recognized. His hair had been cut and hugged his head like a black cap. He wore a well-cut gray tweed riding coat, sleek britches, and tall polished black boots. It was a good thing the night was on the cool side or he would've been roasting.

"Where did you get . . ."

"At the Salvation Army store," Luke grinned. "Me and Perce bought lots of clothes at the one we had in Sully City. Rich folks like yours take stuff to places like that for folks like mine to buy. Once, Miss Hattie had to go to a wedding; she got herself a dress made outa pink beads, and blue shoes and a yellow lace shawl to go with it. She turned out looking prettier'n the bride!"

JoBeth knew what Luke said was true: After the funeral, Mother had gathered up armloads of jackets, plaid skirts, and sweaters of every rainbow color from Ashleigh's closet and took them to a used-clothing store. But now JoBeth had to stare, dismayed, at her own worn jeans and faded shirt. "Compared to you, Luke, I look like . . ."

"Like the poor one and I look like the rich one," Luke finished with a grin. He grabbed her hand and pulled her into the midway. "Quit being so gloomy, JoBeth; tonight we're gonna have fun!"

First, they bought corn dogs and root beer. Later, when they rode the Ferris wheel, Luke pointed toward the Ohio River and the faint lights of Covington, Kentucky, on the far side. "Sully City's only a hundred miles south; I wonder what Miss Hattie's doing right now while you and me are riding this thing?" he wondered softly. "We weren't kin, it's true; but I liked that old gal just the same."

After the Ferris wheel, they had their fortunes told ("You'll meet a tall, dark stranger," the gypsy said, and JoBeth blushed); then, too soon, it was ten-thirty.

"I've got to go," JoBeth said. "My father is waiting for me; I can't make him wait all night."

"Just one more ride, okay?"

"We've already ridden them all, Luke."

"There's one left. I saved it till last because I like it best. Let's ride the merry-go-round, JoBeth." He smiled into her eyes.

Before she could stop him, Luke ran to the ticket booth and bought two tickets. I'm almost fifteen, JoBeth told herself, and it won't be like when I was only six. But she looked with misgiving at the horses whose glass eyes glittered in the reflected lights of the canopy over their heads, at their nostrils flared wide to show painted red linings.

Luke grabbed her hand, and this time JoBeth found herself astride a dapple-gray horse, and Luke was beside her on a chestnut-colored one with a yellow mane and tail. He reached across the space that separated them and hooked his little finger with hers. The merry-go-round began to turn. Luke leaned toward her, but with his chestnut horse moving up as her dapple gray was moving down, the kiss he aimed at her glanced off the end of her nose.

"You know something, JoBeth?" he whispered. "I think I know how people feel when they say they love each other. On account of right now I feel like I practically might love you."

JoBeth was glad the music was loud. It meant she didn't have to try to answer. Because those were words she couldn't give back to him. It would be like tempting fate to whisper, "Maybe I love you too,

Luke." Besides, how could a person tell when she really loved someome?

On the ride back home, Father asked in his mild, sweet way, "Did you have a nice time with your friend, JoBeth?"

"So-so," JoBeth answered. "We rode the merry-go-round. That's for little kids, though; I'm getting too old for rides like that." She leaned against the car window. Across the Ohio River, the lights of Covington softened the night sky with a rosy glow. Too old for the merry-go-round, she realized, but still not old enough to know anything about love.

11

Once, August twenty-first had seemed light-years in the future. To agree to be in a horse show had been easy; then show day loomed closer. Soon it was only a week away. Finally, only hours away.

Each morning for a week the grounds of the Ohio Hunt and Show Club were busier than the day before, as riders and horses began to arrive from towns and countries around Everly. On the morning of the show, JoBeth couldn't practice her routine one final time because by seven A.M. the exercise ring was already full of strangers. Not that she had time anyway, because Luke informed her that both High Pockets and Rye would have to be shampooed.

Luke filled two large buckets with warm water from a spigot at the end of the barn, then got sponges and yellow soap from Mr. Blasing's locker. "I'll start on High Pockets first, so you can see how it's done, JoBeth. We don't have to bathe 'em all over, y'know; just their manes, tails, and legs need washing."

Luke wetted High Pockets' near front leg after lathering his sponge with plenty of hard yellow soap. "This is especially important for High Pockets on account of he's got white socks—and I guarantee when he sashays into that ring tonight, they're gonna look like they've been painted on!"

JoBeth watched Luke scrub High Pockets' legs; he paid particular attention to the horse's heels. Each leg was rinsed until no suds were visible in the rinse water. Meanwhile, JoBeth got two buckets from Ashleigh's locker and started on Rye.

Next, Luke showed her how to brush out Rye's tail and apply some soap, rubbing the tail hairs together to work up a foamy lather. After that came the mane of each horse. Then everything was rinsed with several buckets of warm water. Luke signaled JoBeth to follow him around to the sunny side of the barn. He separated High Pockets' tail into bunches and shook water out of each bunch while JoBeth did the same with Rye.

"Now we'll put on tail bandages so their hair doesn't get frizzy from drying too quick. While their tails are smoothing out, we'll brush their manes." It took an hour to brush the mane of each horse until it was soft and silky. Then the tail bandages were unwrapped and their tails were brushed smooth, too.

Then, beginning with strands of hair close to the tail root, Luke began to braid High Pockets' tail. He lifted strands from each side and braided toward the middle. When that braid was done, he lifted two more strands from each side, lower down, and braided them toward the center, too. He repeated the process from each side, going down about one-third the length of the jumper's tail.

Next, with a needle and thread from his grooming

kit, Luke secured the entire braid by passing the threaded needle through it, wound it tightly around, then tied it. When he was finished, High Pockets' tail, from the root down about twenty inches, looked like a thick, handsome piece of rope.

"Tonight, before we go into the ring, I'll tie some ribbons in it, too," Luke said, eyeing his handiwork proudly.

JoBeth frowned. "How much difference does all this stuff make to the judges? I mean, it seems to me that it should be the ride that counts, not how fancy your horse looks."

"Well, the ride is the most important part," Luke agreed, "but when a judge sees a horse who's well turned out, he knows the rider probably takes just as many pains with his riding." He paused and gave her a shrewd look. "Talking about taking pains—is it giving you a pain to think about riding into that ring come seven o'clock?"

"It is sort of crazy, Luke, you got to admit it. Maybe it happens in movies like *National Velvet*—you know, the plucky little heroine overcomes a mountain of obstacles and comes in first—but I'm not Liz Taylor and Rye isn't the Pi!" JoBeth began to braid Rye's tail. "Besides, I wish the show was being held in the afternoon, like Mrs. Wilson said it used to be. Won't the lights bother the horses?" she asked uneasily. She had had nightmares about it: something would spook Rye, he'd get skittish, and she wouldn't be able to keep her seat, would fall off him right in front of a grandstand full of spectators.

"You don't hafta worry about Rye, JoBeth," Luke said. "He's got a laid-back disposition. Now High Pockets—he's something else. He's still fighting that martingale so hard I decided not to use it tonight. But he still wants to look at the stars, and I could kick myself around this barn for not having drilled him some more over a ground pole."

JoBeth raised her eyebrows and gave Luke a puzzled look. "A ground pole—it's painted a light color so the horse can see it real good—it's laid in front of the jump and clues him when he should start his lift-off," Luke explained. "High Pockets, with his nose in the air all the time, has a habit of lifting off too early, which means the arc he makes over the jump wears out too soon, and he runs the risk of ticking the top rail as he goes over it."

JoBeth was surprised Luke wasn't more alarmed. "Then he could get all tangled up and break the fence and you'd both be . . ."

"Naw, don't worry about that, JoBeth. See, none of the bars on a jump are fixed in place; if he ticks one with a hock it'll just fall right off. But he'll be penalized and won't earn a good score—which is the whole point of me riding him for Mr. Blasing in the first place."

JoBeth glanced at her watch; she wished the morning hadn't gone so quickly. "I have to go home now, Luke. Mother said I should get some extra rest before the show tonight." For an instant, JoBeth was tempted to reach out for Luke's hand. She clasped hers together behind her back instead.

"Remember I told you I was trying to decipher some writing that was carved on the stomach of the stone pony, Luke?" Luke nodded and began to fuss like a mother with one of the braids in High Pockets' mane. JoBeth wished he would stop and pay attention to her.

"Well, that writing turned out not to mean what I wanted it to mean, Luke," she plunged on. "I wanted it to have something to do with the constellation of Orion or the stars in his belt. Only it doesn't, Luke. I guess I've got a knack for wanting things to be a way they can't be."

Luke turned and JoBeth could see that at last he was listening. "What if that's how it is tonight, too, Luke? What if me wanting to be in the Benefit and maybe get a ribbon turns out to be as big a mistake as my so-called hunch about the stone pony?"

Luke balled up his fist and rubbed his knuckles under her chin. "Hey, lady! You're doing your serious number again! You asked once what it'd prove if you learned to ride your sister's horse, remember? 'That you could,' I said. Nobody said anything about a ribbon. You're going out there to ride. Period. Y'gotta trust Dr. Luke!"

JoBeth knew if there hadn't been so many people around, he might've leaned over to kiss her. Instead, he rubbed her chin again. "Stop by Home Sweet Home tonight before the show, okay? I'll give you another pep talk then."

When JoBeth woke up at five, the reason she'd gone to sleep in the first place didn't register right away. It seemed to be a Sunday evening like lots of others. Munchie was barking in the backyard . . . Mrs. Dalrymple was backing her car out of the garage next door and ticked the side of it again with her bumper . . . the strains of a Vivaldi concerto drifted up from the music room.

Then she remembered. *Show night.* Her palms and the soles of her feet immediately got clammy. "Lady, you seem to believe your whole life is a bunch of exams and you gotta get an *A* on every one!" Luke exclaimed one day. "Y'got my permission to do something just because it's fun, JoBeth!"

Easier said than done, of course. JoBeth slid out of bed. She'd laid her clothes across the chair at her desk before she took her nap. Mother had been so thrilled to buy them a person would never have guessed she'd done it before for Ashleigh.

As JoBeth buttoned her cream-colored silk shirt, she wondered if Luke was right about taking exams and getting *A*'s. She tied her green-and-brown paisley print cravat and pulled on a pair of cream-colored gabardine jodhpurs. Next came tall, polished boots. She shrugged herself into her trim new brown jacket. (They'd gone to three stores before finding one small enough in a misses' size.) Last came a brown velvet riding hat. JoBeth cinched its strap under her chin. Then she doused herself liberally with cologne (Misty Morning Meadows, just the right smell for the outdoorsy person she was determined to be).

JoBeth surveyed the result in the mirror on the closet door. Not too shabby. Of course the whole effect might've been more impressive if she was taller and didn't wear glasses. Those two drawbacks went unnoticed by Father and Mother, however, who both seemed dazzled by her appearance.

"You look wonderfully grown-up, JoBeth," Father mused, a halo of pipe smoke crowning his silver curls. JoBeth noticed there weren't any blue smudges under his eyes anymore, that his cheeks didn't have hollows either. "Turn around," he beamed, "and let me look at the whole you."

After she had, Mother leaned over to press a soft

kiss on JoBeth's cheek. "My, you smell positively splendid, JoBeth. Suntan and jokes and now cologne—what'll you surprise us with next?"

How about if I bring home a boyfriend and a blue ribbon tonight? JoBeth thought of quipping, but didn't.

By the time they all arrived at the club, her confidence had already slipped badly. "You guys go find your seats," she urged. "I have to get Rye ready now." What she didn't explain was that first she intended to run straight to Home Sweet Home for a pep talk.

But when JoBeth slid the door of Home Sweet Home aside, it was empty. Not only was Luke not there, his two paperback detective novels and bottle of black hair dye were gone, too. So was the shirt she'd washed for him again two nights ago. The only thing that looked the same was the cot Luke slept on. It was neatly made, as always, and in the middle of the green blanket was a small white square of folded paper.

JoBeth opened it and printed there in a careful, childish scrawl was a message from Luke:

"Dear JoBeth," he began, and she smiled to see how literally he'd taken her name, "that man in the tan car was waiting here for me when you and me finished shampooing the horses. He says he spotted me on the merry-go-round, recognized me even with my rich-person clothes and dyed hair. I'm skinnier by ten pounds than when I ran off from the home, but that didn't save me either. So like I told you, JoeBeth, nothing lasts forever. Just the same, that's how long I might remember you. Your friend, Luke McCafferty."

JoBeth slowly re-folded the note and slipped it into the breast pocket of her riding jacket. She'd never even known his last name. Now he was gone and it didn't matter anyway. She sat down on the camp cot. She loosened her cravat, and the smell of Misty Morning Meadows filled her nostrils.

Dr. Morris had been right; she'd taken a risk with Luke but lost him anyhow. Why did it have to happen again? She'd tried to warn him; but no, he wouldn't listen, had to have things his way. Ashleigh went and got ALL; maybe if she'd been more careful it wouldn't have happened. JoBeth felt hot. Are you angry with Ashleigh for dying? Dr. Morris had wanted to know. *Yes,* JoBeth wanted to shriek, *she ruined everything! And Luke's no better than she was. He deserves to* . . .

As quickly as she'd felt hot, JoBeth felt cold. *To die,* was what she'd meant to say. To realize she could believe such a thing made her feel dead herself.

JoBeth got up from Luke's cot. A headache throbbed behind her eyes. Somehow, she had to get through the next two hours. She couldn't refuse to appear in the ring; her name was already printed in the brochure. Only a person with rotten manners would renege now. Mechanically, JoBeth re-tied her cravat, smoothed her jacket over her hips. Her jaws ached; the skin on her forehead felt tight. She walked out of Home Sweet Home and didn't look back.

JoBeth brushed, bridled, and saddled Rye. She had oiled his hooves after his bath; now she polished them quickly with a clean, soft cloth until each one gleamed. She fished a dozen yellow satin ribbons out of her jacket pocket and tied one to each braid in his black mane. Rye sensed her tension, and even though he was not a horse to get "up" like High Pockets did, there was an eager gleam in his dark eyes. Poor High Pockets. . . .

"Bet I know exactly what you're thinking," came a familiar southern drawl at her back. "Poor High Pockets; now he'll never get those points!"

When JoBeth turned, she knew her mask was firmly back in place. Her face felt like it'd been carved out of stone. It was Luke, all right. He was dressed for the show ring, too, and was leading High Pockets. Behind them both waited the man JoBeth had seen in Mrs. Wilson's office.

"I thought you said in your note . . ." JoBeth began stiffly.

"After Mrs. Wilson explained about the deal with Mr. Blasing," Luke explained, "Mr. Williams here said I could have my turn in the ring tonight. Soon's I finish, though, he's got to take me home to Kentucky."

Mr. Williams stepped forward. He looked as sad and apologetic as Barney, Robin's beagle. "It's the law, miss," he sighed. "If the boy hadn't run off like he did, he'd nearly have served out his time by now. But with him an orphan and all, I reckon he's got to go back, all right."

JoBeth drew herself up as tall and straight as she could. Mr. Williams ought to know he didn't owe her an explanation of anything, least of all the fate that might await a person named Luke. "I'm quite sure you're only doing what you have to do," she said in her chilliest nobody-knows-me voice. When Luke gave her a quizzical smile and reached for her hand, JoBeth lifted it quickly away.

"Excuse me, Luke," she said. "You know my class comes up before yours does. I don't have any time to waste, okay?" She had no intention of getting involved with him again. She gathered up Rye's reins and sailed past Luke and Mr. Williams without another glance.

But in the twilight outside the barn, JoBeth felt suddenly close to tears. *Push, pull; push, pull.* That awful demon she could never run fast enough to get away from was still trying to tear her apart. How many times had she wished she could take Mother's brown fingers in her own . . . or wanted to touch one of those hollow spots in Father's cheek . . . or imagined dropping a hoop over Luke's shoulders and hearing herself whisper, "Ride a winner, Luke!" But she never did. Never could.

Her name didn't sound like her own when she heard it called out over the loudspeaker. The announcer stumbled over it, almost made it Job-eth: "Miss Job . . . *Jo*Beth Cunningham, that is, ladies and gentlemen, riding her nine-year-old gelding, Riono."

Rye pricked his ears forward, and his walk as she rode him into the show ring was crisp and collected. JoBeth halted Rye directly in front of the judges' stand and dismounted. Her toe lightly touched the point of Rye's croup. That'll cost me something, she realized. Then she remounted; that part went smooth as silk.

Rye was on the bit, and by applying only the slightest pressure to his mouth and firming her left leg against the girth, JoBeth urged the horse to step backward. She watched his ears to make sure he didn't turn his head and back up crookedly. No fewer than four steps and no more than eight, Luke had told her. JoBeth backed Rye six steps in a perfectly straight line.

Next, she walked on a long rein, Rye's neck

136

extended, his head free, his gait long and rhythmical. When she tightened the reins, he collected himself smartly and she urged him into a trot. She disengaged her feet from her irons to demonstrate good balance, then engaged them again and posted.

JoBeth completed her figure eights and only had a little trouble with the diagonal lead on the counter-clockwise circle. It had always been her weakest point, and she realized now she should've drilled longer on it. She repeated her figure eights, using a canter as the gait of choice, and finished her routine back in front of the judges' stand. There was a smattering of applause from the gallery, and then contestant number three was called.

There were six contestants in the maiden class. One was a six-year-old boy who rode like he'd been born on a horse. As soon as all entrants had participated, JoBeth rode forward to take her place with the other five in front of the judges' stand to await their decision.

"First place," the judge intoned, his voice hollow-sounding over the microphone, "goes to Mr. Bradley Barrett of Cleveland, Ohio." The six-year-old, mounted on his Cobb-Welsh crossbreed, went forward to collect his blue ribbon. But I knew perfectly well I'd never get a blue ribbon, anyway, JoBeth thought.

"Second place, ladies and gentlemen, goes to Miss Katie Lyn Donoghue," the hollow voice went on. Well. She had thought she *might* get a second place. Katie Lyn, who had been the final contestant, trotted forward to receive her red ribbon from the show steward.

"And third place, ladies and gentlemen, has been

awarded to Miss Job . . . *Jo*Beth Cunningham. It is our pleasure to present this silver ribbon this evening, for we have been informed that its winner has been riding for the very short time of six weeks, and the judges found Miss Cunningham's accomplishment particularly noteworthy." Who'd told them that? Mrs. Wilson? JoBeth trotted forward, too, and received her silver ribbon.

"And now, our first entrant in the hunter-jumper seat . . ." That would be Luke's division. JoBeth hurried out of the ring. She didn't intend to watch. Then, against her better judgment, she scanned the program she'd stuffed in her pocket. Luke's name jumped off the page at her; he was fourth. The first three contestants did very well, and JoBeth knew that Luke would have his hands full bettering their performances.

". . . Lucas Lee McCafferty, agent, riding High Pockets, owned by Mr. and Mrs. Nathan Blasing. High Pockets has collected seventy points, and we will see this evening whether he will move on to a grade two classification. . . ."

The moment JoBeth saw High Pockets she realized Luke might be in for trouble. High Pockets clearly was excited by the lights and moved with more than his usual liveliness. When High Pockets made a final swing before his approach to the first jump, JoBeth could see that his eyes glittered almost as brightly as the eyes of the horses on the merry-go-round. And while Luke had removed the martingale that High Pockets so disliked, she could see that he had cinched the noseband more snugly than usual in an effort to control the big bay's tendency to throw his head into the air.

The first jump was a three-foot straight rail fence. High Pockets cleared it cleanly and with style. Luke seemed hardly to move on the horse's back, so much was he a part of High Pockets' efforts. The second jump was a spread fence, which High Pockets also cleared easily, but JoBeth noticed that this time his nose was even a bit higher in the air. A soft evening wind came up, and JoBeth realized she was perspiring. She loosened her cravat to cool herself.

Just as High Pockets approached his third jump, which was a higher, broader spread than the other two, an empty styrofoam coffee cup was lifted by the wind from a table in the judges' stand and went rolling across the tanbark show ring.

High Pockets caught the movement of the white cup out of the corner of his left eye. He swerved in front of the jump but didn't alter his momentum by so much as a stride. Instead, he bore down full tilt, both eyes now fastened on the high overhead lights, on the fixed, white, six-foot fence around the show ring itself.

Eight feet from the ring fence, High Pockets lifted; his trajectory was short; he caught the top rail of the fence with his left shank bone. The rail splintered with a sound like a human scream. JoBeth saw Luke lose his seat; the reins trailed uselessly from his fingers. His body described an arc in the night air . . . seemed suspended as if by strings from the lights. . . . Then he plunged into the sea of night grass on the far side of the fence.

JoBeth heard a terrible, wrenching shriek close by. Then someone, a stranger, was shaking her by the shoulders. "Miss! Miss! Stop screaming; it won't help, miss, it won't help him now!"

But JoBeth couldn't stop. "It's not fair," she cried, "not fair, not fair!" Ashleigh, from the dock, rose in the air as sleek as a dolphin, traced an arc in the summer air, vanished into the blue lake without a ripple to mark her passing. She'd never held Ashleigh's hand until it was too late; never said *Good luck, Luke,* until it was too late for that, too.

JoBeth dropped Rye's reins into the stranger's hand and started to run across the show ring toward the dark, silent sea of grass on the far side of the white rail fence.

But JoBeth couldn't stop. "It's not fair," she cried, "not fair, not fair." Ashleigh, from the desk next to

12

JoBeth lingered in the fading November sunshine outside Rye's barn. There was no need anymore to hurry. Or be afraid.

She hooked her thumbs in her belt loops and glanced through the doorway at the pigeons roosting in the rafters. They were probably the same blue and green and bronze birds she'd noticed that morning long ago. Except it hadn't really been so long. Only five months had passed since she first stood in this same spot. In a way, she felt like she had right after the funeral, when she began to realize the world had changed and would never be the same again.

What happened after the Benefit made that plainer than ever.

As JoBeth walked toward Rye's stall, her steps were punctuated by the crackle of the letter stuck in her hip pocket, the same pocket in which she used to carry the cuneiform notebook. The handwriting on the envelope was careful and childlike as before.

"Dear JoBeth," he began, having somehow learned

how to spell her name, "Miss Hattie says for me to thank you again for telling Mr. Williams about her. She has got herself appointed to be my guardian and says it don't matter a whit to her if we are blood kin or not. My leg is lots better now. Miss Hattie's got two pigs I tend to, along with taking in the eggs for her. We only got ten acres, though, and don't have any horses. Not that I'll be riding again for a long spell, anyway."

JoBeth had read Luke's letter so often she didn't have to take it out of her pocket anymore to remember almost every word of it. "The court made Mr. Williams my probation officer. I don't have to serve the rest of my time at the boys' home since I'm not an orphan anymore, but I got to report to him every week. He says I should take a test for a GED. That means General Equivalency Degree. If I pass it, it means I'll be sorta like a person who's graduated from high school. I told Mr. Williams I knew a person up there in Ohio who took a test every time she got out of bed in the morning, but he looked at me kinda funny. When you see High Pockets, JoBeth, you tell that old stargazer a styrofoam coffee cup picked up by the wind is no reason to put a guy in the hospital. And Miss Hattie wants for me to tell you that if you're ever in our neighborhood, she'd be glad for you to drop by. Your friend, Luke McC."

Rye heard her footsteps and began to whinny eagerly. JoBeth fingered the key in her right hand. It was dry. Lately, it took something really important to make her hands clammy. She didn't need to debate with herself very long, either, before answering Luke's letter. When she did, she noticed for the first time how much different her handwriting looked: it

142

was just like it used to be, the *l*'s straight up and down, the *i*'s dotted with little open circles. Nobody would ever mistake it for Father's.

"My mom says I might be able to see you next summer," JoBeth wrote. The noun used to be mother. A person could use words as well as gestures to keep a safe distance between herself and other people. "She—my mom, I mean—is a really super tennis player and doesn't look like she's forty-five years old at all. In the spring she's going to judge some high school matches in Louisville. I'm going with her, and maybe I can stop off then to see you and Miss Hattie."

Rye pawed at the floor of his stall and danced up to the wire screen as soon as he spied JoBeth. He pressed his smoky face eagerly toward her. JoBeth tickled his muzzle through the wire mesh. "Hey, horse," she grinned, "you w-w-want to go for a r-r-ride?" Did he remember how panicky she'd been that first morning? Maybe not; she could hardly remember herself.

As soon as Rye was groomed and tacked, JoBeth led him out of the barn and mounted. Everything seemed so easy now; when she got on the scale yesterday, she'd been surprised to see she'd gained three pounds, too. Mrs. Wilson was quick to comment on the difference. "Didn't I tell you riding could be good for the body as well as the brain?" she teased. "I bet you'll want to be in the Benefit again next year."

"No, I don't think so," JoBeth remembered answering. "I really love to ride—but showing and competing aren't really my thing." I don't need to be anybody but me, she might've added: I don't have to try to be like Ashleigh anymore. Or my father. Or anybody else. I don't have to win blue ribbons or worry about

A's or decode script that's carved on a stone horse, either.

JoBeth headed Rye toward the trail marked *Mountain View*. The leaves on the willow and alder trees that she hoped would hide her presence from Luke had all fallen; the caviletti he'd been practicing on that morning had been moved.

JoBeth pressed Rye into a trot and posted easily on his left lead. She signaled him to canter by adding pressure just behind the saddle girth and by maintaining a firm, three-point contact with her knees, calves, and buttocks. As she rocked along, JoBeth wondered if she'd ever be afraid of horses again. But maybe it was like Dr. Morris suggested: maybe horses hadn't been the problem in the first place.

He was very surprised to see her, of course. JoBeth made the appointment herself, after telling Mother what she intended to do. The red-haired receptionist was wearing new glasses; they weren't smoked and didn't have butterflies. Her tan had faded, too. The inside of Dr. Morris's office was still soothing enough to make a person forget why she was there. But when JoBeth sat in the chair across from his desk, she knew *she* was there to get something rearranged. Not her brains, as Luke said; it was that old feeling (among others) of being a nobody-knows-me sort of person that had to be taken care of.

"I didn't want to talk about them—my feelings, I mean—the first time I came here," JoBeth admitted. "It isn't easy to tell somebody you're jealous of a person you're supposed to like. Love, even. And you were right about one thing: I did sort of wish it'd been me who died. I didn't actually *want* to be dead, of course—but it didn't seem right Ashleigh had to be the one. It made me kind of mad. At her. Isn't that weird? Because everything in our family seemed okay until she went and died; there were two people on one side, two on the other. Life was balanced, you know? When she left, though, it got all lopsided. Bent out of shape, as my friend Robin would say."

Dr. Morris smiled. "Will it help, JoBeth, if I tell you that had *you* been the one who'd got bitten by the fourth sign of the zodiac, Ashleigh herself might be feeling like you do right now?"

He was trying to be supportive, JoBeth realized; it was his job. He even remembered she didn't like the word cancer, that she wanted to talk about the zodiac instead. When he just tried to tell her wasn't true, though, Ashleigh wouldn't feel like she did, because they'd always been as different as night and day. One a tall, golden person everybody was crazy about, the other a someone who didn't know even if she liked herself.

"If you've decided you'd like to make some regular appointments, maybe we can talk about some of your feelings for the next few weeks," Dr. Morris suggested. JoBeth sighed. It meant she'd probably have to talk about stuff she ordinarily didn't even like to think about: the dumb letter *x* . . . being so jealous of Ashleigh she practically made herself crazy trying to be smarter . . . feeling like a tourist who ended up in a town she never meant to visit.

"I guess I'd like that," JoBeth said. Soon the future might look almost as inviting as the past used to.

JoBeth leaned across Rye's neck, put him on a looser rein, urged him into an easy gallop. The ends of his coarse black mane stung her cheeks like needles; the cool November wind lifted the hair off the nape of her neck. By the time she visited Luke it might be long enough to tie back in a pony tail. (*His* hair was probably back to its real color now.) By summer she might have contacts, too. JoBeth wondered if Luke would think she had pretty eyes. If he tried to kiss her again, she hoped his aim was better and it didn't ricochet off the end of her nose.

Back in the barn, JoBeth exchanged Rye's bridle for a halter, slipped the saddle from his back, and cross-tied him as Luke had shown her how to do. After she mucked out his stall and spread it with new oat straw, she fixed a fresh hay net, gave Rye a vigorous brushing, and turned him back into his clean quarters. She took up his bucket and, whistling, went to draw fresh water from the spigot at the west end of the barn. She stopped whistling in the middle of a familiar passage. What was the name of it? Ah. "Bridge Over Troubled Waters." Maybe Mother had been right. "Things will be all right," she'd promised Father. Maybe they would.

Funny how much a person could learn when things were bad, though. For instance, if Luke hadn't ended up in St. Ben's, she might never have discovered Miss Malowan wasn't a warrior. Not to know that was partly Miss M.'s own fault, of course. If a person runs around all the time looking invincible, pretty soon everybody figures she is, JoBeth thought. Only a day ago, she'd noticed that if any of the gray hair in Miss Malowan's helmet got loose, it looked springy and curly. Miss Malowan had curly hair, like an ordinary person? It'd been another small revelation.

It was Miss Malowan who drove JoBeth to St. Ben's the day before Luke left for Kentucky; Mother and

Father were both out of town and couldn't take her themselves. They went a lot of places together now. It used to be that Mother went one direction to a tennis match, while Father went the opposite way to attend to museum business.

The parties they had at the house were different now, too: one evening, flushed and looking young, Father danced a Highland fling. Watching him, JoBeth realized she'd always wanted to see him a special way: as a scholar, her best friend, her own private possession. But he wasn't really any different than Luke; he couldn't live in a glass cage, either.

When she and Miss M. walked into the hospital room, Luke was laid out flat as a board on his bed, his right leg supported by pulleys and ropes rigged from a frame that covered him like a canopy. In a cast, in the ordinary light of day, it was hard to remember how opalescent and shiny his bones had looked as they stuck up through the rip in his jodhpurs, how bright the blood around the fracture had seemed on the night of the Benefit. Luke's black hair was spread like an ink blot against the whiteness of his pillow, and JoBeth was amazed to see his cheeks were pink under his tan.

"Hey, I thought I was the only person around here who had a license to blush," she teased.

Luke squirmed and turned pinker. "I never been in a hospital before," he apologized. "Shouldn't be in this one, either. Wouldn't be, if I'd been able to handle High Pockets better'n I did."

"Well, you'll be glad to hear he didn't get hurt bad. The vet had to take a few stiches in High Pockets' nose, though. Maybe that'll teach him to stop looking at the stars!" Miss Malowan stirred at her side, and it was JoBeth's turn to have pink cheeks. "Luke, I want you to meet my friend, Miss Malowan," she said, embarrassed to realize she'd almost forgotten her.

JoBeth drew Miss Malowan closer to the edge of Luke's bed and was surprised to see a certain pair of fierce Amazon eyes had suddenly gotten soft and shiny. "I'm sorry you've had such a bad time, young man," Miss Malowan said. Her voice was quivery and held no echoes of clanking armor.

It's all this whiteness, JoBeth decided. It makes her think about Ashleigh. She reached out to take Miss Malowan's fingers in her own. "Sure, he's had a bad time, Miss M.—but I told him what you told me. 'Life has to go on, Luke'—that's what I told him, because I thought it was good advice."

Later, on the steps in front of St. Ben's, JoBeth discovered there was a second reason to explain Miss Malowan's shiny eyes.

"You never called me your friend before, JoBeth," Miss Malowan sighed. "I always wanted to be, you know; I guess I never knew how." It was a relief to realize Miss Malowan didn't know everything either. JoBeth squeezed her hand again. "That's something we might have to learn how to do together, Miss M.," she said.

JoBeth filled Rye's bucket a scant three-quarters full so water wouldn't spill down her pants leg on the way back to Rye's stall. There was one bad thing about Standard Time: It sure got dark in a hurry. Through the door of the barn JoBeth could see the sun was already a copper disk on the rim of the smooth slopes of the hunt club. When she started down the aisle, she noticed one of its last rays glinted off the brass nameplate tacked to Rye's stall door. The plate gave off a soft burnished glow, like a small lamp.

Maybe next year she'd get a new plate made, one which would read:

Riono
OWNER: Josephine Elizabeth Cunningham.

That way, nobody'd ever get the notion she was a boy.

JoBeth paused a moment in front of Rye's stall: she imagined how her name would look there. She hesitated. A vague sense of apprehension took hold of her. She reached out to trace the five letters of the name Ashleigh had given her horse with her index finger. *Riono*.

She was reminded of how many times she'd traced the marks carved into the stone pony, had pressed her fingers anxiously against them like a person learning to read Braille. Could she have been so determined the cuneiform on the stone pony would spell Orion that she'd been too blind to see something much more important?

R-i-o-n-o . . . JoBeth shifted Rye's water bucket from one hand to the other. His name was made up of five letters, too. Exactly the *same* five letters, in fact, that made up the name Orion.

A draft from the door at the end of the barn brushed the back of JoBeth's neck. The sun had gone down; the brass nameplate lost its lamplike glow. By Christmastime, JoBeth knew, the constellation of Orion would be as brilliant in the Ohio sky as it had ever been over the peaks of the Zagros.

"Ashleigh liked to hear that little story about Orion's belt almost as much as you used to," Father had reminded her. Another memory crept forward: Ashleigh liked to lie on a blanket in front of the fireplace at the cabin on Gull Lake and amuse herself making words out of the letters of other words.

Then, a word like *time* could be rearranged to make *mite; stop* turned into *tops;* even JoBeth giggled when Ashleigh made *rats* out of a *star.* JoBeth stood very still. Why had she not seen it before? She must've been blind. A year before she got ALL, Ashleigh had made one more anagram. . . .

"Let me tell you how I made up the name for my horse, JoBeth," Ashleigh had said in the hospice. "See, I thought it'd be neat if I used the same letters as. . . ."

JoBeth remembered those afternoons when Ashleigh wanted to explain how Rye's name came to be. Dread had closed around her heart; she had tuned Ashleigh out. She had never wanted to believe Ashleigh had dreams of her own to weave around a name like Orion. She couldn't have; we were too different, JoBeth thought. An old, panicky feeling took hold of her. *They hadn't been so different after all.*

JoBeth opened the door of Rye's stall and set his water bucket in its holder. It was Luke who had to point out that Rye was almost the same color as the stone pony; she hadn't wanted to see that, either. "The poor stone pony," JoBeth groaned. "Even if he'd been life-sized and stronger than any of the horses that belonged to the *derebeys,* he still couldn't have carried all my hangups around forever."

Rye fixed her with a soft, dark stare. JoBeth rested her forehead against his neck. His winter coat was thick and warm. It was hard now to remember how cool and safe the stone pony always felt. *Let it go, Joey,* Ashleigh used to say; *let it go. . . .*

"I love you, Ash," JoBeth whispered. It was risky, but she tried the words again: "I loved you, Ash. Deep down, where it's always been so hard for me to go, I know I always did."

When her tears started, they were like JoBeth hoped they would be. They were hot and honest and painful. She put both arms around Rye's neck and held onto him. *Her* was a personal pronoun again, and after awhile, JoBeth knew, she might even get to know who JoBeth Cunningham really was, too.

About the Author

Patricia Calvert, who lives in Chatfield, Minnesota, is a senior editorial assistant in the Section of Publications of the Mayo Clinic. She holds a degree in history and is working on a master's degree in children's literature. She is the author of *The Snowbird* and *The Money Creek Mare,* also available in Signet Vista editions.